CLIMBING THE LADDER

A.E. RADLEY

HEARTSOME PUBLISHING

.

SIGN UP

Firstly, thank you for purchasing *Climbing the Ladder*.

Every month I run a competition and randomly select three subscribers from my mailing list to win free eBooks. These books can be from my back catalogue, or one of my upcoming titles.

To be in with a chance of winning, and to hear more about my upcoming releases, click the link below to subscribe to my mailing list.

http://tiny.cc/ctl

I sincerely hope you will enjoy reading Climbing the Ladder.

If you do, I would greatly appreciate a short review on your favourite book website.

Reviews are crucial for any author, and even just a line or two can make a huge difference.

DEDICATION

I am incredibly lucky to have such fantastic readers who encourage me to write.

This book is dedicated to all of you, but especially to AJ, Miira, Carol, Rachael, Angel, Sharon, and Jenn.

And, of course, dedicated to my reason for everything; Emma.

CHAPTER ONE

CHLOE DIXON HELD onto the handrail above her head. She looked out of the train window at the dark tunnels of the London Underground. A book hung loosely from her free hand. It hadn't managed to hold her interest, or stop her from fretting about her new job, as she had hoped.

She turned away from the window and surveyed her fellow commuters. It had been a while since she'd commuted into Central London for work. She felt as if she had rejoined an exclusive club. A club where getting up hideously early, paying an arm and a leg to travel under the city streets, and wearing uncomfortable work outfits was the price of membership.

Despite the shocking cost of a monthly travel card, she was ecstatic to be back in London. Or, in the rat race, as her dad had called it. As per usual, it had taken her parents around fifteen seconds to turn good news into bad.

Her celebration over getting a new job, working for a company she had dreamed of, was soon extinguished under their barrage of questions. What time would she have to get up for work? How much was the cost of travel? How many extra hours would she be away from home due to commuting?

Chloe shook her head to dispel her parents' negativity. They were good people, just overly practical. She loved them both fiercely, but she was also aware of their pessimistic attitudes. She, on the other hand, tried hard to find the silver lining and keep cheerful. She had a lot to be cheerful about.

She didn't know if it was a result of her getting older, or if the world had turned into a more negative place in recent years. She wondered if curmudgeonly old people had always been grouchy or if it was something that happened to many people as they aged.

Whatever the case, Chloe had decided years ago that she would maintain a positive attitude. No matter what life threw at her, she would smile through it.

The commuter train rattled into a station. The platform was packed with commuters desperate to get on the already-bursting-at-the-steams train. Chloe squeezed herself into a corner as people pushed into the carriage.

Five million souls used the London Underground every day. Or so her dad had told her.

It was getting ridiculously hot and crowded. More people pushed their way on board. A signal beeped, indicating that the doors would soon attempt to close. Everyone took a simultaneous deep breath, as if attempting to squeeze into a pair of jeans from the previous summer. The doors started to close, hitting a tall, bald man on the head. He didn't care, as if this were a daily occurrence and being smashed in the side of the head by an automated door was the price one paid for using public transport.

People leaned over her to grab at handrails, leaving Chloe to stare at a stranger's armpit. The train started to move, causing everyone to lean into the gravitational forces.

Her enthusiasm for joining the morning commuters was already starting to fade. She brought up a mental image of the Tube map. She was close enough to the office to be able to walk if she got off at the next stop. If she could get off at the next stop.

She shuddered at the memory of the poor woman who had tried to get off at Green Park. She'd been so engrossed in her newspaper that she hadn't realised it was her stop until the train doors had opened. She'd tried to fight against the tide of people trying to board the train. It wasn't pretty.

Trying to squeeze her way off of the train and then walking at ground level was definitely preferable to being crushed into the wall of the carriage. Next to a man with an unhealthy-sounding cough. And a woman who had forgotten to shower that morning.

Chloe angled her face away from one armpit and found another straight away.

Definitely getting off at the next stop, she told herself.

On her way through Soho, Chloe opened the door to the newsagent. Before she had a chance to enter the shop, a man walked in front of her.

"You're welcome," she mumbled under her breath.

Hot Monday mornings in London were rapidly losing

their charm. Everyone was overheated and miserable to be going back to work after a weekend in the sun. But Chloe was doing her best to stay cheerful. Today was going to be a great day, she could feel it.

She entered the cramped shop and started to look at the magazine rack. Despite the store being so small, the selection was extensive. Fishing, photography, crafts, pets, and the oddly titled 'women's interests.' Women mainly appeared to be interested in knitting and getting rid of cellulite.

She couldn't find what she was looking for, and so she started to look behind some of the magazines. She stood on her tiptoes and looked at the top shelf. Her eyebrow rose, and she quickly lowered her gaze again. While most of the covers were now obscured, she still got an eyeful of some of the more moderate covers that were allowed to be on display. She swallowed and pushed down the desire to flip through the article about losing cellulite.

She crouched down and started to look at the back of the bottom shelf.

The man who had barged past her to get into the shop physically stepped over her to get out again. He sighed in annoyance that Chloe seemed to continually be in his way. She shook her head at his behaviour and wondered what super important job he must have to act like that.

She returned to looking at the magazines on the bottom shelf, moving some out of the way to see what lurked behind.

Nothing.

She stood and grabbed a bottle of orange juice from the fridge. She approached the counter and put the drink down.

"Excuse me," she said, trying to get the attention of the bored man operating the till.

He glanced up at her. An eyebrow rose, but nothing else was forthcoming.

"Do you have any copies of *Honey Magazine*?"

"*Honey*? Have you checked in cooking? Or women's interests?" He scanned the orange juice. "Three pounds."

"It's not a cooking magazine. It's a lesbian magazine." Chloe handed him a five-pound note.

"Oh, right." He seemed unfazed. He put the note in the till and handed her back the change. "Not heard of it. I can order it in for you, if you want?"

"No, I want a copy now. I work there. Well, I'm starting work there today. I've not read this month's issue because it came out on Friday and I was away this weekend…" She stopped as she realised he wasn't interested in her life history. "You really don't stock it? It's, like, the biggest lesbian magazine in the UK. And Europe."

"Never heard of it," he said. "No one has ever asked for it."

Chloe's heart sank. She was in a busy newsagent in Soho and no one had ever asked for a copy of *Honey* Magazine?

"Try the internet? Or get one from work?" he suggested.

"I don't want to look like I haven't read it," she said.

"Well, you haven't."

"I know that, I don't want them to know that. Are you sure you don't have it?"

"I'm sure, I order all the magazines in myself. We don't have it. As I say, I can order it for you?"

A cough behind her indicated that she was in the way. It was a busy Monday morning and people were in a rush to get to work. Most eager to get into air conditioning and out of the blazing early morning sun. She was surprised someone hadn't climbed over her to be served yet.

She grabbed her orange juice and left the shop. She wandered along the street deep in thought. She didn't expect *Honey* to be one of the shop's best-sellers. But she didn't expect it to be missing in action either.

She'd read *Honey* religiously since she was a teenager. She'd never been in a shop and bought a copy, preferring to have it delivered instead. But her subscription was still being delivered to her parents' house and she'd moved out three months before.

Being at her parents' house for six months while she got back on her feet had been demeaning and exhausting. She thought the break-up had been bad, but the aftermath had been worse. She'd temped and worked all the hours she could during those six months. Partly to make as much money as possible to scrape together a deposit for her own place, and partly to only be at home when it was time to sleep.

Today was the day her life started to get back on track. She was in her own room in a house share in south London, she was starting a well-paid job in digital for a company she had adored for the last fifteen years. No more temporary positions, no more working all the hours she could. It had taken nearly a year, but she felt like she was in a good place again.

She smothered a yawn. Last night had been a sleepless one. She'd tossed and turned for hours as she worried about her first day. Especially meeting all of her new work colleagues. She desperately hoped that she would fit in and maybe even make friends.

The day hadn't been off to the best start. She was sleep-deprived and felt like she could still smell the sweaty odour of the Tube ride. The various armpits she'd stared into would no doubt haunt her dreams that evening.

Not being able to get her hands on the latest copy of *Honey* before work was another blow.

She stopped dead in the middle of the street. She stared down at the orange juice in her hand.

"THREE POUNDS? What a rip-off!"

CHAPTER TWO

THE TALL, sleek, glass-and-steel building that housed *Honey Magazine* sparkled in the sunlight. It was a shared office, Chloe didn't know what floor *Honey* was on, or how big their offices were. She'd never stepped foot in the building before today, her interview having been carried out at a coffee shop.

Her heart started to pound. She tried to take some deep breaths to keep herself calm, but she knew from here on she would just become more panicked. It was a trait she wished she could lose. But a racing heart, sweaty palms, bright red cheeks, and raging nerves were part and parcel of being Chloe Dixon. No matter how much she craved they weren't.

It wasn't just the first day at a new job. It was the first day in a role at which she wanted to excel. For a company she had idolised since she was young.

She knew the team was small, her new boss, the interviewer, had told her as much. But how many co-workers she would have, much less any details about them, hadn't been mentioned.

Of course, she knew some information by looking at the masthead within the magazine, and through a spot of online reconnaissance on LinkedIn. But a handful of names and job titles hadn't given her much insight into what to expect.

She looked up at the hodgepodge of buildings surrounding her. Soho sprawled for a square mile, boxed in between the hubs of Oxford Street, Regent Street, Leicester Square, and Charing Cross Road.

Everything could be found in the packed district. Bars, pubs, and restaurants provided a lively night scene. Theatres and clubs entertained packed crowds until the early hours. Global shopping brands neighboured boutique speciality shops. Hotels, sex shops, international foods all had their place in Soho.

The lively blend of so many different businesses meant that no two buildings looked the same. A 1960s brutalist concrete façade could easily be found beside an ultra-modern office block, or even a chic designer boutique.

Chloe had spent a lot of time walking through Soho over the years, but she never got bored of the area. And she never quite figured out where all the small side streets led to either.

She was going to enjoy working in Soho, the food, the nightlife, the hub of constant activity. When Chloe had travelled to New York three years previously, she'd been shocked to find out that the "city that never sleeps" was kicking out Zs at ten in the evening when she desperately wanted a cup of coffee. That never happened in Soho. Soho was always wide awake, welcoming, and eager to show visitors something new.

It was also home to a number of lesbian and gay bars and clubs, which was why it was the perfect location for *Honey Magazine*.

The ground floor of the building was mainly large windows, tinted so that seeing inside was impossible unless you got very close and cupped your hand to the glass. Chloe wasn't about to do that. She'd seen enough films to know that anyone doing that would be seen by each and every one of their work colleagues and would never be able to live it down.

Instead, she kept her head lowered and walked towards the large revolving door. She slipped into the first available compartment and slowly walked around until she was deposited in the reception area of her new building.

The reception was like so many she had seen before; spacious, mainly marble and glass surfaces. Comfortable chairs and sofas. No personality to speak of.

Worried that her inaction might cause one of the security guards to tackle her to the ground, she pivoted and walked towards the reception desk. As she approached the desk she wondered if someone from *Honey* had remembered to tell reception to expect her. Having to explain who she was would be embarrassing. She joined the queue of people and tried to swallow down her fears.

A woman in jeans and a scruffy T-shirt walked past. Chloe looked down at her summer dress and wondered if she'd overdone it. She hoped the woman worked for another company within the large building. The casually dressed employee entered the revolving door, and a few seconds later another woman appeared wearing a suit that probably cost more than Chloe's monthly rent.

She glanced down at her dress again. Now she wondered if she was underdressed. Maybe everyone at *Honey* was going to be dressed very smartly. Or maybe she was too femme. She'd deliberately only applied a light amount of makeup that morning and agonised over which bag to bring. The leather satchel was the ultimate winner, despite it clashing with the feminine cut of her cream dress. It was bigger than most of her bags, and it added a little butchness to her appearance, just in case she needed it.

Chloe never felt she fit in with the lesbian branding. She had long blonde hair, loved dresses, and if you cut her in half she'd be a perfect cross-section of a rainbow made of glitter. To say she was girly was an enormous under-statement.

But she'd learnt early on that being girly didn't always gel with other lesbians. Her first experience in a gay club was marred when people laughed at her for wearing a ribbon in her hair. An older woman holding a pint of beer and wearing a dirty T-shirt proclaimed, with considerable pride, that she could shower in under two minutes. Chloe had never had a shower less than twenty minutes long in her life.

She'd run from the club and wondered if she was a lesbian at all. She had approached the evening with the hope that she would finally find her people, that she would fit in. It had backfired spectacularly.

It wasn't until the next day, when she had spent most of the morning crying on her bed, that her mum had placed her first-ever copy of *Honey Magazine* on her pillow. That was the day Chloe realised that lesbians came in all shapes and sizes.

The man in front of her left the queue. Chloe stepped forward.

"Hi." She smiled at the woman behind the desk. "Chloe Dixon. Here for *Honey Magazine*. It's my first day."

"Congratulations," the receptionist drawled. "You got a name?"

Chloe's brow furrowed. "C-Chloe."

"Of a person who you are here to see," the receptionist clarified. She didn't roll her eyes, but it was in her tone.

"Oh. Um. Natasha Kerr. She interviewed me. She's going to be my boss," Chloe said. Her cheeks felt warm, and she knew she was starting to blush.

Great, rambling and blushing. Great, Chloe. Well done.

The receptionist looked at her for a little longer than strictly necessary before she picked up the phone and stabbed at the keypad with nails that resembled talons.

"Yeah, I have a Chloe…" She looked at Chloe and raised her perfectly sculpted eyebrow.

"Dixon," Chloe supplied.

"Chloe Dixon. She's here to see Natasha?"

Chloe held her breath. She felt for sure that the person on the other end of the phone was going to say that she'd never heard of her. She looked over to the huge glass revolving doors, and the security guard that stood by them. Would they escort her from the building? Her heart rate spiked again.

The receptionist hung up. "Take a seat, someone's coming down."

She nodded quickly, before anyone could change their

mind or ask her a more complicated question. She spun around and made a beeline for the waiting area, perching on the edge of the nearest seat, ready to get up and go the very moment someone called her name.

The man beside her was having a loud conversation on his phone, something about a job being on his radar and how they'd have to touch base offline. She wondered if the women at *Honey* used corporate jargon. She'd never been great at understanding what it all meant. She thought, for instance, that blue-sky thinking involved going outside to consider a problem in better lighting conditions.

A woman strolled by, her heels clicking across the marble floor. She was dressed in an immaculate trouser suit, her hair was pinned up in an impressive style, and she expertly held a tray of takeaway coffees in one hand. Chloe's eyes widened. She hoped the woman wasn't a *Honey* employee. She definitely wouldn't fit in if they looked like that. And she couldn't hold a tray of coffee in one hand. That was definitely a two-hand job.

She looked at her watch. It was twenty past nine. The email had told her to arrive at nine-thirty. It was a nicety that many British companies seemed to have adopted, allowing the new employee to arrive half an hour later than everyone else, to get their route into work sorted, and to allow the staff to be ready for them when they arrived.

Chloe's anxious side hated it. To her, it meant that everyone else was already there, and that she'd have to walk past them in one go rather than meeting them one at a time as they arrived for work.

"Chloe?"

She looked up and nodded. A woman in her mid-forties

was walking towards her. She was wearing casual black trousers, ballerina flats, and a colourful top. She had messy blonde hair, her glasses were on top of her head, and she was smiling welcomingly.

Chloe jumped to her feet and grabbed her satchel.

"Hi, I'm Wendy." She held out her hand.

Chloe shook it. "Nice to meet you."

"You too, pet," Wendy greeted, her strong Northern accent coming through clearly. "I'm the office manager, receptionist, and general dogsbody. We're all really happy to have you on board. Let's get you set up, shall we?"

Chloe briefly closed her eyes. She seemed to be dressed correctly, and the first person she'd met was lovely. So far, so good.

CHAPTER THREE

CHLOE FOLLOWED Wendy over to the bank of elevators. Wendy pressed the button and they waited side by side.

"Was your journey in okay?" Wendy asked.

"It was good. I took the Tube. I walked some of it," Chloe said. She didn't mention the armpits.

"I walked this morning," Wendy said. "It's just too hot down there when it's summer. I know some of the new trains are air-conditioned but not my line. Mine will probably be the very last one to get it. When I'm retired." She laughed and nudged Chloe with her elbow.

Chloe laughed, too, relieved as some of the tension washed away with the reaction. Wendy had a kind face with laughter lines around her mouth. She knew some people hated the facial dips, but Chloe liked them. She thought of them as a badge a fun person should wear proudly.

The elevator arrived, and they both got in. Wendy selected the third floor. Chloe's heart started beating fast again. Her first time in the *Honey* office was fast approaching.

"So, you were interviewed by Natasha?" Wendy asked.

"Yes. I was surprised I got the job, I didn't think it went well. But she called me the next day and offered me the role."

Wendy dipped her head knowingly. "Yes, Natasha is, shall we say, hard to read. You'll get used to her."

Relief swept through her. During the interview Natasha had been aloof to the point of almost being cold. She hadn't laughed at any of Chloe's jokes. In fact, she hadn't even smiled once, as far as Chloe could recall through her cloud of interview panic.

Chloe had almost run away from the interview, convinced that it was probably the worst in history. When she'd got the call the next day, she'd almost fainted with surprise.

"Did she tell you much about the job? About the company?" Wendy asked.

Chloe shook her head. The interview had been decidedly one-way. Natasha had quizzed her about her experience, her knowledge, and what she would do in any given situation. At the end, she'd asked Chloe if she had any questions. By then Chloe was convinced it was doomed and was desperate to leave.

Wendy tutted. "I suspected as much. Well, there are ten of us in the office, eleven now you have started. Helen is our editor-in-chief, Kim is her PA. You'll love Kim. Then there's you and Natasha in digital. In Editorial you have Pippa and Tess, avoid Pippa at all costs. Fiona heads up sales and marketing; Lucy, Rose, and Darcy are her team members. And then there's me."

Chloe's head spun. She felt like she'd never remember all those names.

"Oh, and we have a few freelancers who come in," Wendy added. "We'll introduce you to them as they do. And then there's investors and our CEO, Christine."

"Err…" Chloe said.

"Don't worry, you'll hear these names plenty of times," Wendy reassured her.

The elevators doors opened. They both stepped out and into a plain-looking corridor. At either end was a large glass door. Three other doors were spaced out along the corridor, all plain white wood that nearly blended into the bland hallway.

Wendy turned left and walked towards one of the glass doors. The word HONEY was etched into the frosted glass.

Chloe hurried after her, still trying to remember all the names she'd just heard in the elevator. She wished she'd written them down.

"Here we are, home sweet home," Wendy said. "Well, reception anyway."

Chloe chuckled half-heartedly and followed her into the room. It was a large area with a long reception desk that held a sign-in book. A cardigan was casually slung over the back of the chair at the desk, which Chloe assumed belonged to Wendy. Behind the desk was a floor-length glass window filling the room with daylight.

She felt the hairs on her arms rise. The air conditioning was a relief from the heat outside. She'd almost forgotten about how blissfully cool offices could be while the city outside sweltered.

There was a small leather sofa against the wall. Above were some large framed prints of *Honey Magazine* covers over the years.

"So, this is reception… where you'll find me," Wendy said. She turned and pointed towards the main office. "Here's where we'll find you."

The office was a large, open-plan space with modern, light-wood desks and bare brick walls adorned with more *Honey Magazine* photoshoots and covers. There were three banks of desks. Each bank contained five desks with four corner desks facing the middle and a bigger desk at the head.

Along two walls, large windows brought in light. Along the final wall was a number of closed doors, presumably leading to private offices and meeting spaces. In front of one of the doors was a number of filing cabinets and a desk, creating a little U-shape of privacy. Chloe assumed that door led to Helen's office and that the desk belonged to her PA. Whatever her name had been.

She clutched her satchel nervously in front of her like a shield. There were a few women at the furthest bank of desks. All the other desks were empty.

"There's a big meeting this morning," Wendy explained. "Come on, let me introduce you to this rabble."

They walked the length of the office. Chloe's palms started to sweat on cue, just as she was presumably about to shake hands with people.

"Girls, this is our brand new digital assistant who is

going to drag us kicking and screaming into the modern world," Wendy said.

The three women were around her age. Two looked like they were at their permanent desks. The third looked like she had pulled up a chair to sit with them.

"Chloe, this is Kim Faulkner, Helen's PA. This is Rose Appleby, our social media assistant. And this is Darcy Quinn, our marketing assistant."

Chloe offered a wave across the desks.

"Great to meet you," Kim said. "Helen's been excited to bring you on. I'll set up a meeting once you have settled in. She'll just say hi, won't take long."

Chloe swallowed nervously. "Sounds great."

"I'm so happy that they've filled your role," Rose said eagerly. "I've been begging for more digital support. I have so many things to talk to you about."

"Let her find her desk first," Wendy said. "And don't forget to loop Natasha in on whatever you discuss."

Rose nodded her agreement. Wendy was clearly a mother figure to the younger members of the office. Although they were all adults, they were probably all under thirty, like Chloe.

"Do you know what's happening in the meeting?" Darcy asked.

"No idea. I think it was a last-minute thing," Wendy replied.

"I saw Celia and Christine go in there," Darcy fished.

Wendy shrugged her shoulders. "When they want us to know, they'll let us know."

Chloe could see that Darcy wasn't convinced. She now

guessed that the three had gathered to discuss what was being talked about behind closed doors.

"It's because the figures were down again last month, isn't it?" Rose asked.

"Figures go up and down all the time," Wendy said. "Just get on with your work and stop worrying about things."

Darcy and Rose swivelled their chairs back to face their desks. Kim stood up and pushed her chair back to where she had gotten it.

Wendy turned around and gestured for Chloe to follow her.

"Never mind them, they are always looking for drama where there isn't any," she whispered. "They are great girls, though. I think you'll all get on brilliantly."

They walked back to the first bank of desks they had passed. Cables sprang up in between the four empty desks. The one at the head was clearly occupied.

"This will be you." Wendy tapped the back of a chair. She pointed to the desk at the head of the bank. "That's Natasha's desk. And the other three are hot desks for freelancers or whoever happens to be visiting. Make yourself at home, I'll just go and get your MacBook out of the cupboard."

Chloe sat at the desk and placed her satchel on the ground. She opened the drawers of her desk pedestal, pleased that she had three drawers. It had been a while since she'd had a desk of her own.

"Hey."

She jumped and spun around to see Kim was sitting on the edge of her desk.

"H-hi," Chloe replied.

"So, Rose, Darcy, and me have lunch together in the staff kitchen at one every day. You're welcome to join us."

"Oh, that sounds great. Thank you. I… I'll have to go out and grab a sandwich."

"Sure, you can pop out and get something and we'll see you after. If you want, I mean we won't be offended if you have other plans. I know some people want their lunch hour to just zone out and forget about work." Kim laughed. She slid from the desk. "Anyway, if you need anything, then my desk is over there, in front of Helen's office. Or drop me an email. Everyone is really friendly, well, except Pippa. And Natasha's a bit weird."

"You're the second person to warn me about Pippa," Chloe said.

Kim folded her arms and leant back onto the side of the desk. She scrunched up her face in concentration. She had the look of someone trying very hard to be diplomatic.

"She's… loud. And rude. Don't get me wrong, she's great at her job. She's just a complete bitch as well. She shouts a lot and doesn't have any issues with calling someone a moron. But she's deputy editor, Helen's second-in-command, so she can kinda do whatever she likes."

Chloe didn't like the idea of a wildcard member of management who might call her a moron. Her face clearly displayed as much. Kim reached out a hand and patted her on the shoulder.

"Don't worry, you're digital. She's editorial. You'll hardly speak to her." Kim leaned back. "You met Natasha, right?"

"Yeah, she interviewed me."

"How did that go?" Kim chuckled.

"It was interesting," Chloe admitted. "I didn't think I'd got the job."

"She's got Asperger's," Kim explained. "She's really good at her job, but the social niceties... not so much. In fact, she doesn't talk to anyone ever if she can help it. Doesn't socialise with anyone. Just comes in... does her work... goes home."

"Ah, I see." Chloe had suspected that Natasha might have been on the spectrum. She had some experience as her cousin had recently been diagnosed with Asperger's.

Things were becoming a little clearer.

While she had nothing against anyone with Asperger's, she wondered what it would be like working for someone who rarely spoke. Chloe loved to chat and laugh at work. It didn't seem like that would be on the cards in a team of two with Natasha as one half of that duo.

Chloe bit her lip. She wanted to ask about the meeting. Clearly Wendy's introduction had interrupted a conversation about it. Kim seemed nice, and Chloe wondered if she may be willing to share some information.

"Was it... Rose? Who was asking about the meeting? Something about figures?"

Kim grinned at Chloe's not-so-subtle fishing exercise. She looked around to check that no one was listening to them.

"Circulation figures and ad revenue are the two main things talked about around here. Both have been going down for a few months now, nothing major. All printed media are having the same problems. It's not a big deal, but Rose worries about things. She'll be banging on about this meeting for days, or until the next drama comes along. I wouldn't worry about it."

"Kim, phone call," Wendy called out from the reception area.

"Better go, catch you at lunch!" she jogged over to her own desk.

Chloe immediately liked Kim. Her concerns about working with Natasha and Pippa were being dampened by the knowledge that there were nice people in the office, too. Wendy was a real mum figure, and Kim seemed sociable and kind. She'd already been invited to lunch, so maybe she would make friends at *Honey*.

She looked up at the closed door to the meeting room and wondered about her other new colleagues.

CHAPTER FOUR

"THERE MUST BE SOMETHING," Darcy said. She flipped through Rose's in-tray again. She didn't understand how someone who worked in social media could have so much paperwork. She was sure that Rose just kept things in her in-tray in order to look important.

"Nope. Nothing urgent anyway," Rose said. She leaned close to the screen and read a Twitter thread. "Why are you so eager to go in there anyway?"

"To see what's going on, of course." Darcy gave up looking. She flopped into her chair, turning back to her desk, dejected.

"You couldn't pay me enough money to walk into that meeting now. All the bigwigs in one room, looking up at you as you walk... Oh! I see."

Darcy winced.

Rose had just caught onto her plan and was no doubt about to tease her mercilessly for it.

"You want to see... Celia," Rose breathed out the name.

"No," Darcy lied. "I want to see if I can see what's going on in the meeting. It's weird that everyone has suddenly gone to an emergency Monday morning meeting. You said so yourself."

The side-by-side corner desks were angled for ergonomic comfort, which allowed Darcy to keep the back of her chair to Rose. A relief, as she knew her cheeks were flushed in a serious blush. She cursed her pale skin for giving her away all the time.

"But seeing Celia would be a bonus, wouldn't it?" Rose pressed.

Darcy grabbed hold of her desk and pulled herself closer. Eager to put a few more centimetres between her and Rose.

She looked at her much-loved postcard of the vintage poster for *Madama Butterfly*. The calming sounds of "Un bel di vedremo" played in her head, and she wished she was at the Royal Opera House. It was a strategy she had used for years. When things got too much for her, she retreated to her favourite place. As far as she was concerned, nothing was more calming than a night of opera.

Rose was right. She did want to see Celia. Darcy would give anything for a few seconds' sight of the woman. Of course, she was curious about the reason for the meeting. But Celia Fox was her primary motive for wanting to gate-crash under the guise of some urgent piece of information that needed to be conveyed.

"I'm sorry," Rose said softly. "I don't mean to tease you."

Darcy turned slightly to face her co-worker. "It's okay."

Rose did tease her, frequently, but she didn't mean anything nasty by it. Darcy was just overly sensitive, and

Rose never took anything seriously. It was amazing they got on at all.

Rose scooted her chair closer. "I just hate seeing you head over heels for someone who doesn't, and will never, know that you even exist. I'm not trying to be cruel, just realistic. It's been a year, and I'm pretty sure she hasn't got a clue who you are."

Darcy snapped her head back to look at her screen. Her emails hadn't changed since she got in that morning, but she stared at them with ferocity. Anything to get away from Rose's look of concern.

Rose was right. Celia didn't know who she was. And why would she? Celia was a non-executive director and investor who only occasionally visited the office. Her role was to provide finance and business consultancy when needed.

Darcy was simply a marketing assistant, the lowest position in *Honey* at present. Even Darcy's boss didn't get to speak to Celia with any frequency. And Celia had no communication with the marketing department at all.

As much as Darcy watched Celia's every move with captivation, it was probably true that Celia didn't know her at all. And, if she did, it was simply as the marketing girl with long blonde curls.

"Maybe you should come out with me this weekend?" Rose suggested. "I'm going out with a couple of friends to a club. I know it's not really your scene, but you never know, you might find your future wife there."

Darcy chuckled bitterly. "I don't think my future wife is going to be drinking Jägerbombs and... body popping... at a club."

She looked up at the closed meeting room door. The person she wanted was on the other side of that door. Completely unaware that she existed.

"Body popping? Wow. Have you ever even *been* to a club?" Rose laughed.

"Once. The table was sticky, so I went home." Darcy took a deep breath. "Do you have anything that I can use to go into the meeting or not? An important message or something I can pass to Fiona?"

"Sorry, nothing." Rose did sound genuinely apologetic. While she didn't agree with Darcy's fascination with Celia, she was generally supportive. Something Darcy was grateful for.

"Fine. Then we'll just have to wait and see what happens." Darcy pulled her keyboard towards her and started composing an email. She'd been happily putting it off for the last three weeks but now seemed like a great time to finally reply. Anything to change the conversation and get her mind off the meeting.

"Kim said she's going to invite Chloe to lunch."

"Hmm?" Darcy asked, still focusing on her email.

"Chloe. New girl."

"Oh, yes." Darcy looked up over her monitor. Wendy was sitting with Chloe, presumably giving her the introduction to the office that Natasha never would. She guessed that Chloe was around the same age as her, approaching thirty. She assumed Chloe wasn't as desperate as she was to get to the arbitrary milestone.

Thirty sounded so much better than twenty-eight. Something seemed to change when someone was thirty, they were considered an adult, despite having legally been one for the past ten years. It was perception. And Darcy knew people perceived her to be young. Her childlike features, her long curly blonde hair, and being under thirty caused people to talk to her as if she were a baby.

"It's going to be good to have a new member of our club," Rose continued.

"We don't have a club."

"We do. It's the young, cool kids club."

"If that's the case, then count me out. I have enough problems being taken seriously around here without being a member of that club."

Rose sighed. "You know what I mean. Everyone else is, you know, older. Lucy, Fiona, and Tess are in their thirties. Pippa, Wendy, and Helen are in their forties. Celia's… old."

"She's fifty-two, it's not that old," Darcy argued. "Not these days."

"More than twice my age," Rose commented.

Darcy turned around and pinned Rose with a glare.

Rose swallowed. "I'm going to…" She pointed to her screen.

"Excellent idea," Darcy said.

CHAPTER FIVE

WENDY PLACED A STACK OF PAPERS, crowned with a MacBook and a coil of cables, onto Chloe's desk. Chloe nearly drooled at the sight of the MacBook. At last, no seven-year-old desktop the size of a set of encyclopaedias.

"Just a few bits of paperwork to go through," Wendy said. She pulled up a chair from one of the nearby hot desks. "Nothing too dramatic. Health and safety, pension forms, next of kin, and the important bank account details for your salary."

Chloe's mind drifted. She'd have to put her mum down as next of kin. It was funny how life kept serving her reminders of broken-down relationships. Five years of putting one person down as her partner, her next of kin, her everything. And then suddenly she was back to listing a parent.

At least I have them both, Chloe comforted herself. She knew many people had no one at all to put on the dreaded form. Still, it was another stark reminder that her life wasn't where she'd hoped and expected it to be. Five years ago, she would have thought she'd be married by now. Now she was living in a house share, half her life in boxes in her parents' garage, eagerly awaiting her first salary so she could feel like a grown-up again.

Wendy organised the papers and put them in a metal in-tray on Chloe's desk. "I'm sure you'll have some time today to fill these in. Just pop them back to me by tomorrow evening. If you have any questions, then let me know."

"Thank you, I'll get them back to you as soon as I can," Chloe promised.

She didn't like outstanding tasks. She'd always been the kind of person who completed jobs as quickly as possible, so they didn't hang over her head like a dark cloud.

Wendy handed her the MacBook and the cables. "I'll leave all of that to you. If you need any help with setting it up, then you can ask Kim. I'm useless at anything technical!"

Chloe chuckled. "Oh, I'll be fine."

"Of course, you're all digital," Wendy joked. "Wires and all that come naturally to you, I suppose?"

"They sure do. I've always been good with technical things," Chloe admitted.

"It's a foreign language to me. My twins are only three and they already know how to use the television better than me."

"My mum's the same," Chloe said. As soon as she said the words she worried that Wendy might take offence at being compared to a woman in her sixties. She glanced at

Wendy, but the admin didn't seem to care, or have even noticed, as she stood up and looked around the office.

"Let me show you around the rest of this place; it won't take long."

"Okay, sounds good."

They walked back into reception.

"Because we don't have the entire floor, we share the bathrooms and the kitchen with another office," Wendy explained.

She opened the door to the *Honey* offices and stepped out into the communal hallway. She pointed to the glass door at the other end of the corridor.

"That's B-Design Architects offices." Wendy rolled her eyes. "They're a little snobby."

Chloe grinned. She could imagine.

Wendy gestured towards a door. "That's the bathroom." She walked farther up the corridor and into the shared kitchen.

Chloe followed her and looked around the room. It was tidy with modern appliances: a large fridge, a kettle, and a microwave. In the corner of the room, by the window, was a round table with six chairs.

"Most people eat at their desks," Wendy explained. "Kim, Rose, and Darcy commandeer the table during lunchtime."

"They invited me to join them," Chloe said.

"Oh, good." Wendy looked genuinely pleased. "I just have a sandwich at my desk, bad habit I know."

Wendy opened the fridge. "We have the top two shelves. It's cleaned out every two weeks on Friday, so if you leave something in there, it will be thrown away."

Chloe knew about strict refrigerator rules only too well. It was a year since she'd lost a fancy salad box to a sudden office clean at an old job. She still mourned it.

Wendy closed the fridge door and opened the cupboard above the kettle.

"Oddly enough, all the *Honey* mugs are ours. Everything else is B-Design's. Now and then *Honey* mugs go missing so I'm sure they are taking them, but they deny it, of course."

Chloe's eyes lit up at the mugs.

"Would you like one?" Wendy asked knowingly.

"Could I have one? Like, to take home?" Chloe would drink out of it morning, noon, and night. *Honey* was a little like a religion for her.

Wendy nodded. "Absolutely. We all have them. Little known fact, the last order was done by Darcy's predecessor. Lovely girl but dumb as a box of rocks. She put an extra zero on the last mug order. That was a year and a half ago and we're still trying to give them away."

"I'll definitely take one off your hands," Chloe said.

"Fab!" Wendy closed the cupboard. "I'll grab you one from the stationery cupboard at the end of the day."

"Bye, Wendy," a female voice called out as they passed the kitchen.

Chloe turned around but just missed whoever it was.

"Bye, Christine," Wendy called out in reply.

She gestured for Chloe to come closer. "That was Christine Thackery, she's the CEO. She manages a few publications under the same umbrella, so she comes in maybe once or twice a month."

"So… she's a big deal?"

"She's *the* big deal," Wendy confirmed. "But you'll probably never deal with her. Helen is the boss as far as we're concerned. But Christine is Helen's boss. Just so you know, in case you see her around."

"I didn't really see her," Chloe admitted.

"I'll flag her up to you next time she's in."

Chloe was glad for the heads-up. It would be just her luck to say the wrong thing in front of Christine, having no idea who she was. That was one of the problems with a new company, it took a while before you knew all the faces. Luckily *Honey* was quite small, so the chances of Chloe making a fool of herself were a little smaller than in a large company.

"That must mean the meeting is over, or nearly over. We better get back," Wendy suggested.

As they walked towards the office, Chloe wondered about Christine's presence and the mysterious meeting.

"So, Christine isn't here often?" she asked.

"Not really, she pops in now and then to see how things are going."

That didn't soothe Chloe's concerns. Wendy seemed to have a knack for making everything sound normal and reassuring everyone that there was nothing to worry about. She probably would have been great on the Titanic.

They walked back into reception. Chloe's gaze immediately gravitated towards the meeting room door. It was still closed. Her earlier fear of having to meet her new colleagues was now replaced with fears over the sudden meeting and news of declining sales figures.

"So…" Wendy walked around her desk and sat down.

"I'm wondering if there's anything else I need to tell you or show you? I feel like I'm missing something."

Chloe shrugged. "Bathroom, kitchen, laptop. I think I'm ready to get going. Well, once Natasha is out of the meeting."

"There's usually a staff meeting every morning at ten. Everyone can get caught up on where the current issue is, as well as any other news." Wendy looked at her watch. "I doubt we'll be having one today."

While Wendy was doing her best to maintain a cool exterior, Chloe could feel the overall tension in the office. This meeting was unusual, and it seemed to have everyone on edge.

The meeting room door opened. The sound of the metal latch scraping against the plate caused everyone to look up anxiously.

A woman stepped just over the threshold. She wore a grey trouser suit and a crisp white blouse, she had short light-brown hair. She looked stunning.

Chloe's eyes widened.

She'd only seen the woman for a couple of seconds and already she could feel the tell-tale start of the knot in her stomach. She found herself staring, relieved that she wasn't directly in the woman's line of vision.

No, no, no, please, no, she repeated over and over in her mind.

But it was useless. Her stomach clenched, and her palms sweated. All signs of the start of a Chloe Dixon crush.

Classic Chloe. The first day at work and already she had found someone to pine over. Probably someone happily married, and definitely unobtainable.

"Kim? Could you come in here please?" the woman asked, a faint Scottish lilt to her voice.

Kim grabbed her iPad, stood up, and followed the woman into the meeting room.

The door closed behind them.

"That was Helen. The boss," Wendy explained.

Damn it.

CHAPTER SIX

Kɪᴍ sᴛᴇᴘᴘᴇᴅ into the meeting room and closed the door behind her. She knew she'd be called in eventually. As PA to the editor-in-chief, it was inevitable.

"Take a seat, Kim," Helen said, gesturing to a vacant chair beside Natasha.

Kim sat down. She set up her iPad in front of her. She glanced around the table at the unhappy faces, trying to get an idea of what was going on.

Celia and Helen sat next to each other on one side of the large, square table. In front of them were stacks of papers, old issues of *Honey*, and spreadsheets.

On the next side of the table sat Pippa and Tess. Pippa looked as pissed off as ever. She was reclined in her chair as if the company didn't deserve her interest. Her jaw twitched as she ground her teeth. On the other end of the editing team spectrum, Tess smiled at her in greeting. Kim smiled back, relieved to see a happy face.

The final side of the table held Fiona and Lucy. Fiona

acknowledged her presence with a slight nod of her head. Lucy remained invested in a piece of paper she was reading.

Kim couldn't blame her. They'd been dating for three months and were still finding their feet on how to act around their teammates. Most of the time Lucy handled the awkwardness by completely ignoring Kim. Some people might have been offended. Kim thought it was adorable. They were lucky to work in a small office with no HR department to speak of.

"Just to catch you up, Kim," Helen started. She handed over a few sheets of paper. "The last quarter figures are down, this time more than we had anticipated. The circulation figures also continue their general trend in the wrong direction. We need to get things turned around before these issues become more serious."

Kim looked at the papers. Red colours and minus figures filled the bottom lines of multiple spreadsheets. Working for the boss meant she was already aware of the financial situation.

It wasn't exactly *Honey*'s fault. The magazine was good, and the quality of articles was better than many competitors. But the printed media market as a whole was in freefall. People were less and less likely to want to buy a magazine, and more likely to want to read on their digital devices.

Sure, *Honey* had a digital edition, but they'd been slow to adopt the expensive technology and were now in a game of catch-up for their lives.

The other major issue was the sheer amount of free content available online. With so many news, entertainment, and review sites all providing their articles for free, why would people want to buy magazines for the same content? Especially when that content was released once a month.

Kim had been watching the steady descent of readership and income since she started. At first, it was simply explained away as "market adjustment." It soon became clear that this was actually a substantial shift in the way entertainment and news was consumed.

While the larger magazines could take the financial knock and move on, *Honey* couldn't. Their market was small, their costs were already barebones. Honey had borrowed from other magazines in the past, but it wasn't a permanent solution. They needed to be solvent in their own right.

It was only a matter of time before some kind of emergency measures needed to be taken. With Celia and Christine organising a last-minute Monday morning meeting, it seemed like now was that time.

"If there are cuts to be made," Pippa interjected, "they won't be found in editorial."

Kim saw Helen take a calming breath. It was clear this conversation had been had a few times already.

"Without editorial, there is no magazine to sell. Fact." Pippa dropped her fountain pen onto her notepad. She folded her arms and looked at Natasha. "If there are savings to be found, I suggest we start with looking at digital, or marketing."

Natasha calmly leaned forward. "Digital is providing a lot of revenue and helping *Honey* to grow. The stats clearly show that the paper edition is moving back, and the digital edition is moving forward. But it's not enough to plug the difference. If anything, we need to be investing *more* in digital."

Fiona nodded her agreement. "Exactly. And without marketing, you'd have no ads, it would be impossible to produce the magazine. Marketing has been stripped back to the bone, we can't run properly as it is."

Pippa laughed loudly. "Let me just count up my department… one moment." She looked at Tess and then pointed to herself. "Two. And marketing has, how many? Four? We have twice as many people trying to sell the magazine as we do trying to make the magazine? That doesn't seem right to me."

"Shall we count how many freelancers you use?" Fiona threatened. "Yes, my headcount is higher, but your monthly costs outstrip mine. The things I could do with your unlimited budget; our issues could be solved tomorrow."

"Thank you, ladies." Helen held her hands up. "We've discussed this enough for the morning. I've brought you all up to speed on the situation. Now, I'd like you to all go away and think about any savings that can be made." She levelled a look at Pippa and Fiona. "Within your own department, please. But more importantly, we need to consider ways to increase circulation figures. Reducing costs is only going to help as a stopgap measure to survive. I don't want *Honey* to just survive; I want it to thrive."

Everyone murmured their agreement.

Helen closed her leather personal planner. "We'll meet again at the end of the week. Kim, can you arrange a time that suits everyone?"

"Sure." She was already accessing the group calendar to see when that would be.

"If you can all submit your plans to Kim before the next meeting, she'll collate, and we'll discuss. Right. Let's get on with making a magazine," Helen said.

Everyone except Helen, Celia, and Kim stood up and started to make their way out of the room. Pippa was the first out of the door, mumbling under her breath as she did.

"Thanks for coming," Helen said to Celia.

"My pleasure. I'll get you those market reports I mentioned, fascinating reading," Celia replied. "I'm sure we can use some of the examples to turn things around here."

"Will you be joining us for the next meeting, Celia?" Kim asked, her finger hovering over the button to send the invites.

"Send me an invite, if I can make it, I will," Celia replied.

Kim made a mental note to tell Darcy that Celia might be making an appearance in the office that day. She'd never hear the end of it if she didn't give her some warning.

"Will I see you at the National Gallery on Wednesday?" Celia asked Helen.

"No, I received the invitation, but I can't do Wednesday," Helen replied. "But I'll see you at Margo's party in a couple of weeks."

"Fantastic, looking forward to it." Celia looked at her watch. "Where does the time go? I better make a dash, call me if you need anything. Bye, Kim."

"Bye," Kim said as Celia hurried from the room.

Helen gathered the papers and placed them on top of her planner. She walked out of the room towards her office.

Kim followed her. She could feel Rose and Darcy's eyes

on them as she walked into Helen's office and closed the door behind them.

"It's not serious," Helen said. She sat at her desk and kicked her heels off. "Not yet, anyway. But it could be."

"Christine's not happy, I bet?" Kim asked. She sat in one of the chairs in front of Helen's desk.

"She's not doing cartwheels, no. It's bad timing; all of the other titles are doing well or holding their own. We stick out like a sore thumb, fifth month on the trot with an overall decrease." Helen let out a sigh and ran her fingers through her short hair.

"Can I do anything?" Kim asked.

Helen shifted her head from side to side. "Book me an appointment with my masseuse. I have more muscles knotted than unknotted at the moment."

Kim made a note on her iPad.

"We need to keep the office jolly and upbeat. I don't want people talking about the situation if at all possible. If people worry about it and talk about it all the time, the misery will spread, people will leave, and the magazine will die." With a sigh, she changed the subject. "Speaking of misery, can you contact my ex and tell her that I need to move that divorce meeting? Of course, she's booked it for when she knows I'll be preparing for awards season."

Kim grinned. "Sure, I'll drop her an email. She loves hearing from me."

"Almost as much as she loves hearing from me, I'm sure." Helen chuckled. "Did I spy the new girl out there?"

"Yep, Chloe Dixon."

"Make sure to help her settle in, we don't want Natasha to scare her off before she's finished her first day."

"Already invited her to lunch. She seems nice. Do you want to meet her?"

Helen nodded. "Sure, wheel her in and I'll do my standard welcome speech. Whenever you can fit it in the schedule today. Natasha is right, digital is the way forward. We need that department to grow."

"Don't let Pippa hear you say that," Kim joked.

"Pippa would be happy if we went back to the way things were twenty years ago. Digital editions, tweeting, SnapChat… the whole thing gives her a headache. Oh, warn new girl about her as well."

"Already done. And it's Chloe."

"Chloe," Helen said slowly. "Chloe. I'll try to remember."

CHAPTER SEVEN

CHLOE WATCHED as five women filed out of the meeting room. She recognised only the tall, black woman who had interviewed her: Natasha Kerr. The other four women took their seats at their respective desks.

Natasha walked over to her.

"Good morning. I see you're all set up?"

Chloe stood up, expecting a handshake greeting. "Yes, Wendy helped me out."

"Good." Natasha sat at her desk.

Chloe frowned. She looked at the newcomers to the office, wondering who they were and if she'd be introduced to them.

Two of the women, who had sat at the marketing bank of desks, were talking with Rose and Darcy. After a few seconds, they all walked into a meeting room. The other two women sat at the bank of desks next to her. She presumed they were the editorial team, one being the dreaded Pippa.

She looked at Natasha who was already engrossed in her screen. It seemed that introductions weren't happening. She sat down.

"You will need to get InDesign set up on your Mac," Natasha said. "It's the only thing not included in the standard build."

"Oh… Okay."

Natasha picked up a sticky note from her monitor and handed it to Chloe. "This is the number for our IT team."

Chloe took the note. "Okay. Do I… just say I'm from *Honey Magazine*?"

Natasha looked at her blankly for a moment. "Yes. Let me know when your Mac is set up and then I will start showing you through our systems." She turned away and focused her attention on her screen again.

Chloe turned back to her Mac and looked down at the note in her hand. She'd expected a little more guidance, but apparently, she was being thrown in the deep end. She wondered if Natasha was trying to test her initiative. Or if she simply expected Chloe to get on with things with minimal instruction. Either way, it was going to be interesting working for her.

"Hi!"

Chloe turned around. A woman in her late thirties with long, black hair stood in front of her with her hand out.

"I'm Tess Arnold, thought I'd introduce myself."

Chloe stood up and shook her hand. "Chloe Dixon."

"Great to have you with us, Chloe. I'm the features editor around here. And this is Pippa Wilson, deputy editor." Tess gestured towards a fearsome-looking woman.

Pippa looked up and offered her a tight smile and half

nod before returning her attention to her work. The brief greeting was a relief.

"Sorry for eavesdropping, but I hear you're going to call IT?" Tess asked.

Chloe nodded. "Yeah, something about InDesign…"

"When you call, ask to speak to David. He's our account manager."

Chloe sighed in relief. "Thank you," she whispered.

Tess smiled perceptively. "No problem, just speak to David and tell him you need a typical editor set up and he'll know what to do. Any issues, let me know and I'll give you a hand."

"David, got it. Thanks so much."

Tess smiled and patted Chloe's shoulder reassuringly. "You're welcome. I'll catch up with you later in the week, once you have settled in. Explain what we do and how we all work together, that kind of thing."

"That sounds great."

Tess went back to her desk.

Chloe was quickly realising that Natasha wasn't going to be the fount of all knowledge that she'd hoped for. Making friends with other members of staff, figuring out what they did and how she could work with them was all going to be up to her.

CHAPTER EIGHT

FIONA STOOD, leant on the top of the high-backed meeting room chair, and looked at her assembled team.

"I'm not supposed to tell you this," she began, "but I'm going to because I think it's important that you know."

"We're closing, aren't we?" Rose asked, always the worrier.

"No. But figures are down, again."

Rose nervously drummed her fingers on the arm of her chair. Darcy didn't respond to the news. Fiona didn't know if she was simply more adept at taking on bad news, or if her family wealth put her above worrying about employment.

"So, you're not supposed to know," Fiona continued. "But now you do. I'm telling you because I know that rumours will begin to swirl if I don't. It's not fair that some of the office knows, and some doesn't."

"And rumours are always worse than what is actually happening," Lucy added.

"And Pippa is dying to see our budget slashed, so she can take some of it for editorial," Fiona said. "That's not happening, not on my watch. *Honey Magazine* needs a strong marketing team if it's going to ride out this financial blip."

"Is it a financial blip?" Rose asked. "I heard that all magazines are in trouble these days."

"Magazines have to adapt to survive, that's true. It's not like it was ten years ago, even five years ago. Readers have access to a huge amount of free content. And they want it now. To be honest… paper is dead, it's just taking a long time to get in its coffin. While it's still around, we need to support it, but the future is digital. As a department, we need to be trying to route people towards it, more so now than ever."

She pulled out the chair and sat down. "Lucy, I don't need to tell you that we have to increase ad revenue."

"I already have some ideas on that front."

Fiona smiled. The can-do attitude was one of the reasons why she had promoted Lucy to advertising manager.

"Fantastic. We need to play hardball. No more offering discounts just to fill the pages, I'd rather cut the size of the magazine than devalue our offering at this point."

"But isn't some money better than none, for ad space?" Rose asked.

"Not necessarily. Our advertisers talk to each other. If one pays three hundred pounds and finds out that someone else paid a hundred, they'll expect that discounted rate as well," Darcy replied.

"Quite right," Fiona said. She'd always been impressed with Darcy's marketing instincts. The young woman was wasted as a lowly marketing assistant. Fiona hoped that she would get an increase in budget in order to promote her, before the girl got bored and left.

The board had finally seen sense a couple of years ago and started to put more money into the marketing budget. They'd woken up and realised that magazines didn't sell themselves. The market was competitive, and those who spent money made money. Fiona had finally been given the means to grow her team, but there was still a long way to go. She needed further investment to make a real difference. But with cashflow being an issue, she'd have to work with what she had.

"I'm going to speak with Natasha, see if we can get an increase in some of the digital advertising rates. It's the way things are going anyway, so we might as well get started," Lucy added.

"Perfect." Fiona turned to Rose. "We need to ramp up our social media engagement. I know that we've come a long way since you started working on our social channels, but we need to get to a level of engagement that our competitors have. See what they are doing, and other brands. Come up with an action plan."

Rose practically vibrated with excitement at the idea of a new social media campaign. *Honey* had been very slow to get on social media, and, when they did, it had been amateurish at best. Getting someone in to focus on that part of the marketing mix was key to Fiona's future plans.

"Sure. I'll speak with the new digital girl, Chloe. She

must have some ideas for getting more digital subscribers through social media."

"I'm sure she will," Fiona agreed. "And she might need a friend if she's working with Natasha."

Rose nodded emphatically. "We've already invited her to lunch with us."

"Good." Fiona couldn't imagine working with Natasha day in, day out. Her own team could be a little rowdy, and sometimes she wanted a moment of quiet. But she'd rather have that than Natasha's frosty demeanour.

She'd given up trying to make friends with the woman. Or any connection at all. She was impossible to talk to.

"I'll speak to Nicola the next time she is in," Rose added. "See if she can give me some more free stock photos. Our image library is getting a bit repetitive, and if I increase how frequently we are posting, it will be really noticeable. She gave me some free images before, ones that are fine for social media but not good enough quality for sale."

Fiona felt her cheeks heat at the mere mention of the freelance photographer. She looked down at her notes to hide her face.

"That's a good idea, I need something new for my email banner to prospects," Lucy added.

"I hate that one of the woman running through the field," Darcy said. "Why are so many of our stock images women in fields?"

"I know, right?" Rose added. "Why are all these gorgeous women out in the middle of nowhere?"

"Maybe they're responsible for crop circles," Lucy joked.

Fiona let them continue talking about the stock image library as her mind wandered to Nicola Martin. Nicola had been working with *Honey Magazine* forever, offering her work at severely discounted rates while her career flourished. At the top of her career, and only in her mid-thirties, she cut an impressive figure.

As a freelancer, she came and went as she pleased, a motorcycle helmet on a hot desk the first indication that she was in the office.

Fiona has spent the last two years staring longingly at Nicola but was terrified to make a move. Every single time she interacted with her, she said the wrong thing. It was a special gift. One which she was desperate to return to sender.

Time and time again, Fiona had tried to connect with the woman only for it to end in spectacular failure. The most famous, and mortifying, time was when she had attempted to enquire about Nicola's weekend, only to find out that her grandmother had died. Apparently, everyone else knew. But Fiona waded in without a clue and embarrassed herself.

For the final time.

After that, she gave up.

It wasn't like she was great at socialising anyway. At work, she was fine. In an office environment there were rules and obvious conversations to be had. But once out of work, things went wrong. She could no longer predict which direction a conversation might take, and she'd find herself lost, spluttering out the first thing that came to her mind. Never a good idea.

"So, should I ask Nicola to come in for a meeting with us?" Rose asked, shaking Fiona from her thoughts.

"Yes, by all means, drop her an email."

Fiona had a love-hate relationship with Nicola coming into the office now. On one hand, she was happy to be able to see her and stare longingly at her from a distance. On the other, having given up any hope of having a normal interaction with the woman, it was a little like standing outside a closed ice cream shop on a hot day.

CHAPTER NINE

DARCY OPENED her Joseph Joseph lunchbox and unclipped the plastic fork from the lid. Rose was on a phone call, Kim was on her way, and Chloe had popped out to get a sandwich. It was decided, by Rose, that Darcy should go and claim their table. Just in case one of the architects saw an opportunity to snatch it and upset their lunchtime routine. Although she'd like to see the brave outsider who would dare to sit at their table in the shared kitchen.

She stabbed a piece of farfalle pasta and ate it. Her eyes wandered to the hydration tracker app on her phone that sat by her water bottle. She'd been so busy that she was well behind her goal.

Kim had laughed at the hydration tracker when she'd first brought it into the office. Darcy knew she would. It was a present from her stepmother, who was obsessed with any modern tech when it came to health. But Darcy had ignored Kim and relished in the device's news on her daily water intake.

Except for days like today, when she was woefully short of her goal. The morning had gone in a flash. At first, they were worrying about the meeting, and then Rose had been dominating her time with her expectations of *Honey*'s demise.

Darcy had lost count of the number of emails Rose had sent her listing suitable jobs that she had seen online. Rose loved *Honey*, but she also loved shopping. With financial difficulties in the air, Rose already had one foot out the door. And she was encouraging Darcy to do the same.

Darcy had no intention of leaving. If *Honey* ever closed, she'd help whoever was left to lock up the building. The work wasn't the most mentally stimulating, but the people and the ethos of the company would keep her at her desk until the last second.

Kim hurried into the kitchen with a pre-packaged sandwich and a bag of crisps.

"Sorry I'm late." She chucked the items on the table and pointed to the kettle. "Tea?"

Darcy shook her head. "No, thank you." She shook her water bottle.

"Drunk enough decilitres today?" Kim joked.

"No, actually I'm very behind," Darcy admitted. "It's hard to take a sip of water when you have to constantly reassure Rose that the world isn't ending."

"So, Fiona told you guys everything?" Kim guessed. She pulled a *Honey* mug from the cabinet.

"Yes. And, of course, Rose is panicked."

"Rose was panicked before she knew what was happening. Which, by the way, is nothing. Yet." Kim filled up the kettle and turned it on. "By the way, I shouldn't tell you this because it's only encouraging you... but you're my friend so here it goes. Celia told Helen that she's going to the National Gallery on Wednesday evening. Some event, I think?"

Darcy dropped her fork into her pasta salad and grabbed her phone. She closed her hydration app and opened the gallery website. The moment it loaded she checked the events calendar.

"You're wasting your time," Kim told her. "She doesn't know you exist."

"She will when she bumps into me on Wednesday," Darcy told her.

She wasn't entirely sure about that, but she liked to present an air of confidence. Kim and Rose already thought she was insane for pursuing Celia. She had to pretend that she knew what she was doing to save face.

"Who bumps into you?" Rose asked as she entered the kitchen.

"Celia. She's at an event on Wednesday and Darcy is going to *bump* into her. And then Celia will know who she is," Kim explained when Darcy remained silent.

Rose sat beside Darcy. "I've said it once, I'll say it again. You're wasting your time."

"Thank you for your valued opinion," Darcy snarked.

"Seriously. You're going to get old waiting for her to even look at you. There are plenty of fish in the sea," Rose said.

Darcy completed purchasing her ticket for the event on Wednesday and lowered her phone.

"Actually, there aren't plenty of fish in the sea. Being a gay woman, looking for another gay woman, is hard. I know we work with primarily gay or bi women, but the rest of London, the rest of Britain, is predominantly straight. So, finding a woman who you're interested in is bloody hard work for most gay women. But for me, someone who doesn't fit in anyway, it's impossible. How many gay women do you know who love opera? Who spend their evenings reading Virginia Woolf or practicing cello? For me to find someone who shares my interests, who is also gay, is like striking gold while buying the winning lottery ticket."

Rose looked at her blankly. "You really spend your evenings reading Virginia Woolf?"

Darcy rolled her eyes.

Kim returned to the table with a freshly brewed cup of tea. "I get what you're saying. But Celia… she's…"

"Old," Rose supplied.

"Well, yeah," Kim agreed. "I mean, I've seen bigger age gaps, but… I just don't get it."

Darcy closed her eyes and counted to five. She opened them and took a deep breath. She knew her colleagues had been dying to have this conversation for months. She didn't usually explain herself, but they were helping her in her possibly futile quest to spend more, or any, time with Celia. So, she supposed they deserved an honest reply.

"When I first saw her, she'd spent the morning at the Tate Modern. She made a joke to Helen about one of the installations, which I overheard because I was in reception at the time. It was subtle, thought-provoking, and elegant. The next time I saw her, she was on the phone to her friend speaking about the latest run of *La traviata* at the English National Opera. She spoke about it as if she were composing wedding vows."

She opened her water bottle and took a sip.

"Since then I've learnt so much about her. She's on the board of directors for three charities, charities that I have always admired. She has a house in the south of France, literally ten miles away from where my grandfather's house is. Her favourite meal is beef bourguignon, same as me. She played the piano at a friend's wedding because she is so accomplished at it, it's on YouTube and it's…" She let out a sigh at the memory. "It's beautiful."

Darcy sucked in a gulp of air. The truth was hurtful, but she was big enough to admit it. "I know she doesn't know who I am. If she has any idea at all, I'm the 'girl in Fiona's team'. She probably sees me as a child. But I see her as… the only person I could ever really love. It's not a crush. I mean, I can see that she's an extremely attractive woman, I'm not blind. But it's not looks and money. It's her interests, her passions, her *mind*."

Kim grabbed her arm and leaned her head against her shoulder. "Naww, that is so cute!"

"That is kinda cute," Rose admitted.

"Yes, well, now you know." She leaned her head on Kim's. "Thank you both for helping me, even if you do think it's ridiculous."

"I don't think it's ridiculous," Rose clarified. "I just don't want you to get hurt."

Kim sat up. "Same. I don't want you to get your heart broken."

Darcy was sensible enough to know that was probably where things were heading. But she couldn't help herself. She was in love. She had to do whatever she could to try to get Celia to see her. If she didn't try, she'd never forgive herself.

Thankfully, Chloe chose that moment to enter the kitchen.

"Yay, you made it." Kim pulled out a chair. "Come and take a seat with us cool kids."

"I don't think cool kids call themselves cool kids," Darcy pointed out.

Kim ignored her. "How's your first day going?"

Chloe sat down and unpacked a shop-bought salad and an orange juice.

"Yeah, it's going well," she said. "I got my laptop set up, filled in a million forms. Haven't actually done any work yet, but Natasha's not really given me anything to do."

"You need to tell her, repeatedly, that she has to train you and give you tasks," Darcy explained. "Or she'll treat you like decoration and then wonder why her workload isn't going down."

Chloe ripped open her salad. "Yeah, I'm going to bug her this afternoon. Luckily, I used a lot of the same systems in my previous job, so the learning curve should be pretty easy."

"Cool, you'll pick it all up quickly then," Kim said. "And if you have any questions you can always ask us."

"Just don't leave," Rose said. "This place desperately needs to be more digital. I swear Pippa would get rid of the app and social media if she ever got her way."

Chloe chuckled. "I've been wanting to work at *Honey* for years; I won't leave unless they kick me out. As long as I don't mess up for the next three months, you're stuck with me."

Kim wrapped her hands around her mug and leaned back in her chair. "I suppose we should update you on all the office gossip. So, as you already know, Natasha is a little… weird. She's nice enough, but she's hard work."

"We've all tried to be friends with her, but she doesn't want to socialise with any of us," Rose added.

"I didn't want to socialise with these two either," Darcy joked. "I had no choice."

Rose gently elbowed her. "You love us really."

Darcy smiled. She did. Becoming friends with Rose and Kim was one of the best things she'd ever done.

"So, Kim is dating Lucy," Rose announced. "*Honey* doesn't mind employees getting together, as long as they leave any drama at home."

Chloe looked confused. "Lucy?"

"Advertising manager," Darcy supplied. "Sits next to Fiona, who is the marketing manager."

"Oh yes. Sorry, I'm terrible at names. I'll get there in the end," Chloe apologised. "So, you and Lucy, that's cool."

Kim blushed and looked down at her tea. Darcy felt jealous that Kim's blush was easily absorbed by her dark skin. Her own blush could be used to guide aircraft down.

"And Darcy's head over heels in love with Celia," Rose added.

Darcy kicked her under the table.

Chloe laughed as Rose jumped a couple of inches in the air. "Who's Celia again?"

"She's our non-exec director," Kim added. "I think I already told you to avoid Pippa?"

Chloe nodded seriously. "Yeah, I've heard that from a few people. Tess introduced me to her, she looks…"

"Grumpy?" Kim guessed.

"Miserable?" Darcy asked.

"Fucking terrifying," Rose added.

"Yeah, all three," Chloe confessed.

"You shouldn't have much contact with her," Darcy said. "She doesn't like digital things, or anything that's new and modern. So, hopefully she'll leave you alone."

"Yeah," Kim agreed. "Who else? Well, my boss, *the* boss, Helen…"

"Helen's cool. She's going through a divorce at the moment, so she's a bit stressed at times," Rose divulged.

"But she's really nice," Kim added.

"You would say that, she's your boss," Rose pointed out.

Darcy realised that they sounded like terrible gossips and were only dragging up people's dirty laundry. "Tess and Wendy are very nice," she said, trying to add an air of positivity to proceedings.

"Yes, Tess seems really nice," Chloe agreed. "And Wendy, too."

"I hope everyone stays," Rose said. "You know, considering the fi—"

Darcy kicked her teammate again. She smiled sweetly at Rose, trying to convey that telling the new girl about the failing magazine was probably not wise. Especially if she wanted the new girl to stay.

"Considering the fact that salaries are so low," Kim added with a smile.

"Exactly," Rose added.

Chloe looked at the three of them with a smile that didn't quite have Darcy believing it. It had been a strange morning. Darcy wouldn't be at all surprised if Chloe was already attuned to the atmosphere that had pervaded *Honey*. But for the meantime, she seemed happy enough to smile and nod at them.

Give her time, Darcy thought. *If she's smart, she'll figure things out for herself.*

CHAPTER TEN

KIM STARED AT HER SCREEN. The shared calendar wasn't helping her provide a small window for Helen to say hello to Chloe. She reached for a piece of chocolate and popped it in her mouth.

She groaned at the sweet taste and shifted happily in her seat. Her job could be pretty stressful at times. She knew that soothing herself with sweet treats wasn't the healthiest way to cope, but it was certainly the most enjoyable.

Something caught her eye and she looked up. Helen was passing her desk, bag in hand and summer coat draped over her arm.

"Are you going out?" Kim asked. She looked again at Helen's schedule. She was supposed to be in all day. Busy, but in the office.

Helen paused and turned back to face Kim. "Yes, I have that meeting with Tom about the print changes. Did you need me for something?"

"It isn't in your calendar." Kim looked up at Helen.

Helen bit her lip. "Oh, yes." She smiled sheepishly. "It was moved from tomorrow to today. He emailed me yesterday, I thought I updated the appointment. Clearly, I didn't."

If Helen controlled her own calendar, nothing would ever be noted down. And she'd forever be double-booked.

"Sorry, Kim," Helen apologised. "It has to be today. Have I caused disaster?"

Kim's lips curled into a smile. "Not quite. I'll move your afternoon appointments around. I was just looking at your schedule to see when you had five minutes to say hello to Chloe."

Helen frowned. "Chloe?"

Kim raised an eyebrow and stared at her forgetful boss. She wasn't going to remind her, she'd get there in the end.

The penny dropped, and she snapped her fingers. "Oh, new girl. Chloe. Yes, Chloe." Helen turned around and looked at the main office. "I'll say hello to her now, that will be that done."

"Okay. I'll sort out your schedule for today and I'll leave remembering that Chloe exists and saying hello to her to you," Kim said.

"Chloe…" Helen said distractedly. "I'm going to have to remember that."

She walked off to say hello to her newest employee. Kim sighed and shook her head. How Helen managed to run the company was sometimes a mystery.

She was an excellent editor, a fantastic journalist, and a legendary LGBT+ rights activist. But how she remembered people's names, where she lived, or whether she'd eaten was a total mystery.

It wasn't that she didn't care about people. You didn't

take an underpaid job at a struggling lesbian magazine when you could be making five times as much elsewhere if you didn't care. Helen just always seemed to be thinking of fifty things at once. Details like remembering to eat lunch or go home were irrelevant to her.

Kim's predecessor had told her that Helen needed someone who was mix between a personal assistant and a carer. Kim had laughed, but on from the first day she had realised it was true.

Helen may have been her boss, but in many ways, Kim felt like Helen's mum. Despite being eighteen years her junior.

She reached for another piece of chocolate and watched as Helen weaved her way through the office. She approached Chloe's desk from behind. Chloe jumped out of her seat as Helen said hello.

They spoke for a few moments. Helen seemed to do most of the talking while Chloe nodded, her face red and a look of mild panic about her.

Must be nerves, Kim thought. While she never thought of Helen as particularly scary, she was the boss.

After a few moments, Helen stepped away and waved goodbye to everyone for the day and left the office.

Kim set to work rearranging Helen's afternoon appointments. It wasn't the first time she had had to throw out a whole afternoon's worth of meetings. And it wouldn't be the last.

From day one, Kim had access to Helen's calendar and her email account. The idea being that it would allow Kim to manage Helen's time and keep up to date with where she was and when. But Kim didn't always feel comfortable looking at Helen's emails, especially lately with the divorce happening. Spiteful emails from Helen's ex and financial information from her legal team were things that Kim wanted to avoid.

Kim had explained early on, and Helen had immediately understood. She explained that she'd do her best to keep her calendar up to date, but it was likely, probable even, that she'd fail from time to time. In those instances, Kim had her blessing to go into her email account and correct whatever appointments she needed to.

She trusted Kim and Kim was grateful to have that trust.

Of course, it didn't help that Helen approached technology like a toddler confronted with a snarling dog. She stabbed in confusion at buttons on her smartphone screen and had only recently mastered the swipe action needed to answer a call.

Kim opened Helen's email and immediately found a few meeting requests that Helen had failed to deal with. She reached for another piece of chocolate. When she couldn't see her toes anymore, she would blame Helen.

She started to move meetings around, adding in the ones that Helen had ignored or attempted and failed to deal with. She moved around internal meetings to accommodate things, waiting for Pippa to start shouting at the last-minute changes. Kim thought she would be used to it by now. Everyone knew that if you had a meeting booked in with Helen, it was about a fifty-fifty chance it would go ahead.

She was about to click out of Helen's emails when she noticed a new email arrive. It was from Christine and the subject line caused Kim's heart to stop for a split second.

Headcount

She paused her movements. Her mouth went dry as she debated what to do. Christine wasn't emailing to ask how many people worked at *Honey*, she knew that already. There was only one reason Christine would email about headcount: to reduce it. There was interesting information within that email, Kim just knew it.

She stretched a little higher and looked over her monitor. No one was looking at her. She lowered back down again.

She tugged at her lip. Just because no one was looking at her didn't mean it was right. It was clearly an email that Kim shouldn't see. It was marked private with the pointless little red exclamation mark that did nothing to protect it from prying eyes.

Kim swallowed. She'd never thought of herself as prying eyes before. She sat up again, the coast was still clear. She had to know. Her hand was moving the mouse before her brain really had time to think about what she was doing.

She clicked the email and looked at the preview box below.

Helen,
I know you wish to focus on an increase in readership rather than a decrease in expenditure, but I feel an easy solution, for the time being, would be to make Lucy Bryce redundant and use an external outsourcing firm for advertising needs instead. A few of the other publications have done this, with much success.

I'll call you to discuss.
Christine.

Kim read the email three times. Each time she expected the contents to change, but of course they didn't. She clicked off of the email and marked it as unread. She hurried to close the inbox.

She let out a deep breath and leant back in her chair, putting some distance between her and the message. Of course, it made no difference, she'd done the deed, she'd read the email. But quickly removing it from sight and adding a few centimetres between her and it was soothing.

But it was short-lived.

Now she had to decide if she should tell her girlfriend that she was about to be made redundant. She shook her head. The answer was obvious. Of course, she would tell Lucy, there was no way she couldn't. She had to warn her. Lucy wasn't exactly flush with cash and losing her job was a huge deal.

The thought of breaking Helen's confidence was soul-destroying. Helen trusted her, they were as close as a boss and personal assistant could be. And Helen was a great boss, a great person.

Kim reached for another piece of chocolate. With her arm outstretched, she stopped herself. Instead she swept the remaining pieces of chocolate into the bin. She didn't deserve a treat. She'd done something terrible.

CHAPTER ELEVEN

Chloe rushed into the restaurant. She was ten minutes late, which wasn't bad considering. She'd texted ahead to let her family know, but she knew her brother would still reward her tardiness with the stink eye.

Apparently, it was fine for Chloe to spend endless hours listening to their parents' nonsense without another human being for support. But Kevin liked to keep family gatherings as brief as possible. He socialised with them when he absolutely had to, not a second more.

"Sorry I'm late," she announced, dropping her bag and her coat onto the vacant chair. She leaned down and kissed her dad on the cheek. "Happy birthday, Dad."

"Thanks, sweetheart," Dad replied.

She kissed her mum on the cheek and then sat down next to Kevin. She certainly wasn't going to kiss his cheek. Or look at him at all, if possible.

"We waited to order," Mum said.

"Oh, I said to go ahead without me," Chloe replied.

She'd been looking forward to a shorter meal as a result. She hadn't exactly wanted to go to dinner the evening after her first day at a new job. Though she couldn't say no to her own father's birthday dinner, she could attempt to shorten it a little, so she could rush home and fall into bed in an exhausted heap.

"We wanted to wait so we could hear all about your day," Mum explained. She lowered her menu and looked at Kevin. "It was Chloe's first day at the lesbian magazine."

Kevin slumped in his chair. "I know, Mum." It clearly wasn't the first time it had been brought up, probably not even the seventh time.

Chloe hated being the centre of attention. Especially when her brother was in the room. They'd never gotten along, and he mocked everything she did and was interested in. The moment her parents shone a spotlight on her, she felt defensive. She knew it was only a matter of time before he said something, and she'd have to explain herself and her life choices.

"I'm going to get some drinks," Dad announced. He stood up. "Beer, Kev?"

"Please."

"Chloe? Wine?"

She shook her head. Alcohol would surely see her asleep before dinner was served.

"Can I have an orange juice?"

Dad frowned. "You mean a J2O?"

"No, I mean an orange juice."

"Like, a Fanta?"

Chloe shook her head. "No. An orange juice. The… juice… of an orange."

"You don't usually drink that," he told her.

"I… always drink that." She'd been alive for twenty-nine years, and her own father had no idea of her favourite drink. She shouldn't have been surprised, both her parents had an uncanny knack of tuning out anything they didn't find interesting. Which was most things that didn't directly involve them. They weren't bad people, just self-centred.

He shrugged his shoulders in defeat and walked towards the bar.

"How was the journey to work? Was it horrible?" Mum asked. She'd never been one for optimism.

"It was… busy," Chloe confessed.

"I'm having a burger, what are you having, Mum?" Kevin asked, trying to move the subject and the whole evening on a few steps.

For once, Chloe was in agreement with him. The sooner they ordered food, the sooner the whole dinner process would happen, and the sooner it would be over. But their parents were too cunning for that, they would delay ordering as long as possible to keep them as prisoners. It was a rich person's interrogation. If you want dinner, you'll answer all our questions.

"Salmon. Are there any nice girls at your office?" Mum asked, zeroing in on Chloe again.

"Um. Some. I… I've not really met everyone yet."

"Is your boss nice?"

"She's… okay."

Mum frowned. "What's wrong with her? She's not one of those bitchy businesswomen, is she?"

Chloe chuckled. "No. She's just a bit quiet. I think I'm her first employee, so we're just settling in, you know?"

"Is she single?"

Chloe rolled her eyes. "I have no idea."

Probably, she thought. She couldn't imagine someone living with Natasha, unless that person also liked hours of stony silence.

"Does she have a name?" Mum asked.

"She does…"

"What is it?"

"Why do you want to know?" Chloe picked up the menu, trying to deflect her Mum's laser vision.

"Because she's your boss. You'll talk about her, and I'll think, 'Oh, yes, that's Chloe's boss.'"

"You'll think that if I say, 'my boss.' You don't need to know her name," Chloe pointed out.

"She wants to know so she can Google her," Kevin interjected.

"I don't Google people." Mum sounded just scandalised enough to have been caught in her devious plan.

"You always Google people," Dad said as he returned to the table with the drinks.

"Shush, you," Mum said. She shook her head, convinced that Dad alone was the reason for her masterful plan's failure. She picked up her menu.

"Wine, wine, beer… and orange juice," Dad said as he placed drinks in front of the family. "How was the first day of work?"

Kevin sighed. "We've done that bit. It was fine, she's not met everyone yet, she won't tell Mum her boss's name, and the commute was busy. Which is code for hell on earth, because that's commuting into London. Are we ready to order?"

"What Kevin said," Chloe agreed, anxious to move the topic on.

"Good, you've been angling to work there for years," Dad said, as if she didn't know. Her father had a strange habit of telling her things that she had previously told him, as if it were ground-breaking news.

"Yes, I'll enjoy it while I can," she said.

Mum's radar pinged. She looked up at her again. "Is something wrong?"

"No, well… I don't know. They said something about circulation figures being down. I don't think the magazine is doing very well."

It felt a relief to say the words out loud. Clearly no one in the office was too keen to talk about it with her. Natasha wasn't that eager to speak full stop. But the moment the words were out of her mouth, she realised she'd picked the wrong audience.

"You should have taken a job in a steadier sector," Kevin told her, always on hand to dish out life advice despite being a useless twit.

"She was offered a job at one of the big accountancy firms. Lots of letters. BEO? ED?" Mum started guessing various letter combinations.

"I didn't want to work for an accountancy firm," Chloe defended. "I wanted to work somewhere that makes a difference."

"Won't make much of a difference if it goes under," Kevin muttered.

"PUD? BBD?" Mum continued.

"Well, you know what you have to do, don't you?" Dad leaned back in his chair. He had a suggestion that he assumed would fix everything. But Chloe knew he was waiting for her to ask for his pearl of wisdom. Dad didn't just say things, that was far too easy. He made cryptic statements that forced the other person to have to ask for clarification.

Most of the time that led to him either mansplaining something, or worse, telling her something that she'd previously told him. But on rare occasion he had something worthwhile hearing. And so, Chloe always asked. Just in case.

"What?" she asked.

"You need to save the company. If they are going under, you need to stop it from happening. You work in marketing—"

"I work in digital," she corrected.

"So, you can market the magazine and bring in a load of new money. Within the year, you'll run the place."

"I don't work in marketing," Chloe clarified.

"Well, you can still save the business." Dad picked up the menu. He wasn't going to quibble over the details of his plan. As far as he was concerned, Chloe would save the company with her marketing prowess. Despite not having anything to do with marketing.

How he still had no idea what she did, she didn't know. But then he didn't know her go-to drink was always orange juice.

"JBO?" Mum asked, still on the letter conundrum.

"Jesus…" Kevin mumbled under his breath.

CHAPTER TWELVE

Chloe picked up her notepad and pen. She stood up and brushed any creases out of her dress. She took a deep breath and prepared to psych herself up for what was coming.

It was her first meeting at *Honey*. Which meant it was her first opportunity to shine. Expectations were high. With the company in trouble, and digital seen as a lifeline, all eyes were on her and Natasha.

She followed Natasha into the meeting room and took a seat at the table, watching as everyone else entered and started to take their places.

Dad's words from the previous night were ringing in her ears. Of course, he felt she was able to do anything, he was her father. It was in the job description. She was surprised he hadn't sent her to the Middle East to "sort it out." His endless faith in her was heart-warming.

It was also completely misplaced.

The problem was, Chloe had two modes: blurting out

stupid statements, and enormous attacks of shyness that prompted total muteness.

These two modes increased in intensity and likelihood in stressful situations. Such as sitting next to Pippa Wilson, who had yet to utter a full word to her, and opposite Helen Featherstone, her boss's boss. The editor-in-chief of her favourite magazine ever. And someone who Chloe could very much find herself with a crush on.

So far, Chloe had only interacted with Helen once. It was a short hello and welcome to the company. A handshake which had left Chloe trembling. It had been one of Chloe's mute moments, so she nodded and giggled, presumably making herself appear an absolute idiot. Something she hoped to rectify at this meeting.

She'd seen Helen around the office just a handful of times and already she was hooked. Helen was a powerhouse of energy. She was short, wearing heels to compensate. She dressed in suits that demanded respect and attention, and Chloe gave both willingly.

Having only recently gotten over her previous relationship, Chloe suspected that she was simply crushing over an unreachable goal. Helen was older than her, more accomplished than her, and would unlikely see Chloe as anything other than the new digital assistant. It was a safe crush. One she could enjoy from the comfort of her own desk without any chance of anything happening.

She'd convinced herself that it was her swirling emotions looking for an outlet. Her relationship had been all-consuming. Coming out of that had been hard, she'd felt like half a person for the longest time. All the love she had put in was now homeless and in need of a direction. A harmless crush wouldn't hurt anyone.

Chloe felt like she had definitely drawn the short straw, as she sat between Natasha and Pippa. Lucy, Rose, and Darcy all sat in a row to her right, the latter two offering her a smile of support. Fiona, Tess, and Kim sat to her left. Helen sat dead opposite Chloe, a whole side of the table to herself. Anyone else of her stature might have looked dwarfed, but Helen commanded the space she was in.

"Good morning, everyone," Helen said. She shuffled some papers in front of her. "We have a lot to get through, so let's get started. Features?"

Tess leant forward. "We've got some great pieces coming up. My favourite is coming in from Zahara this afternoon, on queer-baiting vs. searching for subtext that isn't there. We're finishing up on the article about gender-neutral clothing that we spoke about last week. I'm tempted to move that to next issue though?"

"To pair it with the casual weddings piece?" Helen asked. She removed her glasses, popping the end of the frame into her mouth as she looked at the ceiling, deep in thought. "Yes, I like that. Move it up to next issue. Any ideas on what to replace it with?"

Tess gestured towards Pippa. "Pippa is able to stretch out her interview with the top five business women, pad it with some of the photos that Nicola took."

"Whoever voted them the top five women in business and why is quite beyond me," Pippa finally spoke. Her tone was deep, and her accent was from the posher parts of the south of England. She reminded Chloe of a stern head-mistress she had once had.

"Are you happy to take up the page space?" Helen asked, ignoring the comment.

"Yes, I'm sure I can pick through the carcass of the interviews and find something that relates, however vaguely, to business. I can't tell you how many of them immediately dove into talking about clothing, hair, makeup. As if the cover is more important than the mind." She tapped her head with her index finger.

"It's presumably what they're primarily asked by mainstream media," Fiona pointed out.

"I don't care. Until we start acting and speaking like the professionals we are, we are going to be reduced to talking about what shade of lipstick we're pairing with our handbag." Pippa snorted a derisive laugh. "Just because we're women doesn't mean we have to be done up like Christmas presents, primped and perfect. Style over substance."

Chloe shifted uncomfortably in her seat. She'd put on another summer dress and cardigan combination. She wondered if Pippa was about to round on her and point her out as an example of a woman in business consumed with her looks.

Pippa wore a casual linen shirt and khakis, clearly valuing comfort over style. Chloe wished she were brave enough to say that she didn't dress up for anyone, she did it for herself. She enjoyed wearing dresses, just as Pippa seemingly enjoyed wearing khakis. Why did someone have to be right and someone wrong?

"I can do both," Helen said. "And, sometimes, I have to dress a part to be taken seriously. I'm not saying it's right. But it's a fact of life for many women in the workplace, especially in a city like London."

Pippa's face flared red. Chloe instinctively slid a little closer to Natasha, fearing an eruption.

Helen held her hand up. "But that's a topic of discussion for another day. We'll move gender-neutral clothing to next issue and you'll take up the two pages with the top five women in business article. Sorted. Where are we on the cover photo?"

"Nicola's coming in with a few options for you to look at," Tess said. "We have some nice shots of the top five women, we think it's probably best to use that."

"Sounds good. I look forward to seeing the options. How is everything else coming together content-wise?"

Tess nodded and looked at the paperwork in front of her. "We have all the reviews in: book, television, movie, and theatre. We're waiting for a couple of images for upcoming media. Culture and events are done and in final checks."

"I'll have them done by the end of the week," Pippa added.

"Great, anything else from editorial?" Helen asked.

Tess shook her head. "Nothing that can't wait until layout."

"Good, good." Helen turned to Fiona. "Marketing?"

"We're working on increasing ad revenue this month. Lucy is spearheading a new campaign. That will obviously take a while to filter through, so we're hoping to see results from that within the next two to three issues." Fiona read from her notepad as if reporting on a military campaign. "Rose is going to be liaising with a few people to create a new engagement strategy for our social media channels."

Pippa laughed sarcastically.

Helen cast her a withering look.

Fiona ignored the interruption and continued on. "We're looking to increase our presence across the board. Because, as we *all* know, visibility leads to interest, leads to sales."

"Fantastic work, Rose, I look forward to hearing more. When do you hope to get some results?" Helen put her glasses back on.

"It's hard to say," Rose admitted. "I need to get the campaign and the assets together and then launch. Hopefully that won't take too long, I'd expect to start next week and see results within a week."

"Or two," Fiona added.

"Fabulous. I look forward to my Twitter followers increasing," Helen said with a grin. "If only I knew what to do with them once I got them."

"Delete your account," Pippa murmured.

"But then I wouldn't be a cool cat," Helen said with mock seriousness.

Pippa's lips curled up in the first genuine smile Chloe had seen from her. She was impressed at how Helen managed to handle Pippa. There was obviously mutual respect there.

"In other news," Fiona continued, "Darcy and I are working on the email rebrand for the digital edition. I'll be speaking with Natasha and Chloe on that over the coming weeks."

Helen turned from Fiona to Chloe. "Wonderful. I'm sure everyone has already met Chloe, if not… here is Chloe. Welcome to the *Honey* team, we're thrilled to have you on board."

Her heart rate spiked at the sudden attention. "Thank you," she whispered.

"Speaking of digital," Helen said. "Natasha? Do you have an update?"

Natasha started to speak, but it sounded like she was in another room. Chloe had become so panicked when Helen had looked at her that all of her senses numbed. She did her best to look like she was listening to Natasha's report. But in truth, she was cursing herself for already being so paralysed with fear that she could hardly speak.

She was lucky that it was her first meeting, and she didn't have any update to give. She was just decoration today. Pippa would have loved to hear her describe herself as that. But the next few days had to change. She had to find her confidence, had to show that she had something to contribute.

As her dad had said, she had to save the company. Then everyone would see her as the essential part of the *Honey* team that she desperately desired to be. And maybe Helen would smile at her again, sending her weak at the knees. Because harmless crushes were safe.

An hour later, the meeting was finally over. Chloe strolled back to her desk, berating herself at having contributed so little. She'd basically said five words the entire meeting. She knew it was her first week and she'd be forgiven, but she still had dreams of saying something masterful and impressing everyone, except Pippa, with her amazing knowledge.

She reminded herself that her time would come. She

needed to settle in. Once she knew more about the business, she'd make her move and do something great.

She dumped her notepad and pen on her desk. The hot desk beside hers held a motorcycle helmet and a MacBook. A leather jacket was draped over the back of the chair. She looked around the office, but there was no sign of the owner.

"Nicola," Natasha said, sitting down at her own desk.

"I'm sorry?" Chloe asked.

"Nicola Martin is in." Natasha nodded her head towards the hot desk. "She's our primary freelance photographer."

"Oh, cool." Chloe sat down. She looked at Natasha expectantly. Natasha logged onto her computer and started to work. The conversation was clearly over. Still, Chloe felt pleased that they had come on in leaps and bounds.

She smiled to herself at Natasha's behaviour and unlocked her own computer.

"Chloe. Digital girl, right?"

She turned around. A tall, blonde woman in jeans and a loose t-shirt with a band logo that Chloe wasn't cool enough to recognise walked towards her. She was smiling brightly and held her hand out in greeting.

Chloe stood up and shook her hand. "That's me."

"Great! Welcome to the team. I'm Nic, if you need anything relating to photography then I'm your woman." She reached into the pocket of the leather jacket on the back of the chair and handed Chloe a business card.

"Thank you." Chloe looked at the card enviously. "I love photography. I mean, I know I'm useless at it, but I love it."

At university she had studied programming, marketing, and photography, hoping that her skills would improve enough for her to become professional. Sadly, she just didn't have a grasp on the technical details, and it never happened.

"No one is useless at photography," Nic reassured her. "It's in the eye of the beholder. An interest is enough."

Chloe chuckled. "You wouldn't say that if you saw some of my stuff. I studied at university, but I had to drop out."

Nic dropped herself into her chair and swung her feet up onto the desk.

"Drop out?" She gasped scandalously.

Chloe sat back down. "Yeah, I took on too many classes. Had to drop one, it ended up being the thing I was bad at!"

"I want to see this terrible, dropout-worthy portfolio," Nic said. "Bring it in."

Chloe blushed. "No way, it's really bad. I'm not even kidding. I thought I was artistic and deep…"

Nic laughed. "Yeah, we all go through that phase. Seriously, bring something in. I'd love to look at it. Not to laugh at—well, that too. But if you have a genuine interest then I might be able to give you some hints and tips. If you're passionate about it, then you shouldn't let a bad experience put you off."

Chloe hadn't thought about photography for a long time. After she'd left the course, she'd sold her camera, boxed up her portfolio, and never really looked at it again. She didn't have a professional camera anymore, but she was forever playing with the settings on her smartphone. Technology had moved on so much that the quality was amazing, there were even movies being filmed entirely on iPhones these days.

She loved her digital work, but the call to do something creative had always been at the back of her mind. Even if it was as a hobby. And now, being single, she definitely had time for a hobby.

"Okay," she agreed. "But I'm warning you. My teacher left, I think she had a breakdown."

Nic smiled. "I love a challenge!"

CHAPTER THIRTEEN

Darcy looked up at the laughter coming from the digital department. She let out a soft sigh. While she was glad that Chloe was making friends with Nicola, she also knew that it would make her day impossible.

She subtly glanced up and, sure enough, Fiona was staring daggers at the laughing couple. She rolled her eyes and opened up a new email to Rose. Despite Rose sitting next to her, they often emailed each other. Fiona's hearing could put dogs to shame.

I think you should go and get Nicola before Fiona implodes. She's here to talk to us anyway.

She sent the email, and out of the corner of her eyes, she saw Rose open it. A moment later, Rose pushed her chair away from her desk and got to her feet. She strolled over to the bank of desks and leaned her arms across Chloe and Nicola's chairs and started to talk to them.

Darcy stood up to reach for something in her in-tray. She glanced at Fiona as she did. Fiona's jaw was tight as she glared at her monitor, clearly pretending to be unaffected by the friendly chatter going on. Darcy sat back down.

She wondered if her crush on Celia was as transparent as Fiona's crush on Nicola. She hoped not. She hoped she wasn't sending laser beams out every time Helen touched Celia's upper arm when they shared a joke. She bristled. In truth, the action was most annoying, she wished Helen wasn't so tactile.

She wished Fiona would just get herself together and go talk to Nicola. She clearly had feelings for the carefree photographer. Yet she spent her time stewing alone whenever Nicola was in the office.

It was ridiculous, Fiona had a chance at happiness. There was nothing stopping her from speaking to Nicola and finding out if there was anything there. If there wasn't, Fiona had the opportunity to move on with her life.

She glanced at her boss again. She was attractive. Not as attractive as Celia, in her opinion. But she was sure that many women would consider Fiona to be beautiful. If rich brown eyes and glossy black hair were their thing. And Fiona was intelligent, cultured, and had a good job.

She looked over at Nicola and decided that she would be lucky to be with someone like Fiona. Darcy liked Nicola, she was funny and lively. She wasn't someone she'd ever consider dating, but Fiona clearly liked her. And had done for some time if the temperature plummeting in the office every time Nicola appeared was anything to go by.

Something had obviously happened to turn her usually confident boss into an uptight, frightened mouse every time she was around. Darcy didn't know what that was, but she wished it would end. One way or another.

She focused on her work again. It was none of her business. If Fiona wanted to let happiness slip by without doing anything, that was up to her. Darcy wasn't about to make the same mistake. She'd make sure that Celia saw her somehow. Even if it meant finding out that Celia didn't want anything to do with her, at least she'd know. She wouldn't waste her life.

Of course, she wasn't going to stalk her. Much. She wasn't a complete freak. She knew not to go to Celia's house, which she had found through online records. But bumping into her at public events and in the office, that was perfectly acceptable.

A loud laugh echoed across the office. Apparently, Rose had decided to join the conversation rather than break it up.

"Darcy," Fiona snapped. "Go and get Rose and Nicola so we can start this damn meeting."

Darcy stood up.

Yes, her day was going to be hell.

CHAPTER FOURTEEN

"I'LL BE BACK in around an hour," Helen told Kim as she breezed past her, bag in hand.

"No problem." Kim smiled.

The moment Helen was out of sight, the smile fell away. Her stomach clenched and churned with stress. She hated that she had broken Helen's trust in her. She hated that Helen had no idea that she had done so. If Helen knew, it would undoubtedly be horrendous, but at least she'd be punished for her actions. Keeping the secret was somehow worse than being caught.

She'd tossed and turned all night, thinking about what to do. On one hand, she wanted Helen to trust her. On the other, she wanted Lucy to trust her. Either way, she was going to have to upset one of them.

Kim couldn't lie. If Lucy were made redundant and she asked Kim directly if she had known, she knew it would be written all over her face. It was still early days, but she was falling in love with Lucy. It wasn't the right time to say so, but she knew in her heart that it was only a matter of time until she did.

But all of that would be over in a flash if Lucy found out that Kim knew her job was in trouble and didn't say anything.

On the other hand, Helen was her boss. Someone who could make her daily life a living hell, if she wanted. Not that Helen would ever do something like that. Which made it all the harder to break a confidence. Helen was the best boss she'd ever had. The thought of Helen being disappointed in her was heart breaking.

But Lucy came first. And, Kim reasoned, Helen never had to know. If Lucy found another job and left, it would help everyone. Lucy would be out of the literal firing line, and Helen wouldn't have to act on Christine's suggestion. The only person who would suffer would be Kim, as she wrestled with keeping the truth from Helen.

She looked over the top of her monitor. Darcy was herding Rose and Nicola into a meeting room. Fiona was picking up her notepad and preparing to follow them in. Now was her chance.

She got up and picked up a folder, doing her best to try to look official. She walked over to the marketing desks and sat at the empty one beside Lucy.

"Hey babe," Lucy greeted, still focusing on typing an email.

"Hey. I… I need to talk to you," Kim whispered.

Lucy's hands paused on the keyboard. She looked around the office in case anyone was listening in. "What's wrong?"

They hadn't been together long, but Lucy was very

adept at picking up Kim's feelings. She instantly knew when something wasn't right.

"I know something," Kim admitted. "But you can't tell anyone."

"Okay," Lucy agreed. She leaned in closer. "What's up?"

"I... saw an email I shouldn't have. Well, I have access to the mailbox so technically I can view the emails in there... but I generally don't. It's not a personal email account as *such*, but—"

"Kim, breathe," Lucy said.

Kim sucked in a quick breath. "I saw an email from Christine to Helen. She suggested making you redundant and outsourcing your role."

Lucy's already pale face became ghostly white. She opened and then closed her mouth, processing the news.

"I don't know if Helen's even seen it. And if she has, I don't know if she plans to do anything about it. She's been dead against losing staff members. But Christine is CEO, she could technically overrule any of Helen's decisions," Kim waffled on. She wanted to give Lucy time to process.

"Wow, right... Okay," Lucy said. "I literally spent the last hour telling Rose to stop looking for new jobs because we're all safe here."

"You can't tell anyone that you know," Kim repeated.

"I know, I know. I won't, don't worry," Lucy reassured. She placed her hand on Kim's thigh. "Thank you for telling me. I really appreciate the heads-up. I know it wasn't easy."

Kim brushed a lock of auburn curls behind Lucy's ear. "Come over for dinner tonight, I'll cook."

Lucy smiled and leaned into Kim's hand. "Not tonight, how about the next night? I'd be rubbish company. I need to get my CV sorted out and start looking for new jobs. I can't afford to be out of work, my savings account was eaten up by car problems last year."

Kim nodded in understanding. "Okay, the next night. I'll make that curry you love."

"Aw, look at the lovebirds," Tess joked lightly as she walked back from the photocopier.

Kim chuckled. They both sat up and waited for Tess to pass by.

"If you need anything, let me know," Kim said. "And remember—"

"Don't say a word, I know," Lucy promised. "Thank you for telling me, I know that must have been really difficult."

Kim tried to shrug nonchalantly, but she knew Lucy would see right through her.

"I promise I won't say anything. Helen won't ever know," Lucy reassured her.

Kim nodded. She didn't know how to explain that there was a part of her that wanted Helen to know. A part of her that hated secrecy and lies. She'd rather deal with the fallout than with lying further. Most people would be delighted to get away with it. But Kim's moral compass was spinning around like a gyroscope and it made her sick.

CHAPTER FIFTEEN

CHLOE SENSED A PRESENCE BEHIND HER. It felt menacing. She imagined it was what the heroine in a horror movie felt when she was being watched through a window.

She turned around. Unsurprisingly, Pippa stood behind her. Arms folded and looking irritated.

"I want to speak to you about some issues with the digital edition," Pippa announced. She turned to Natasha. "Do I speak to you about them, or her?"

Chloe bristled at being referred to as "her." And being spoken about as if she wasn't right there. She hoped Natasha would deal with Pippa and tell her to learn some manners while she was at it. She looked at Natasha, begging with her eyes to be rescued.

"You can speak to Chloe about that," Natasha said before returning her attention to her work.

Traitor, Chloe thought.

"Right, well, the page flip on the digital edition is broken," Pippa said. "It needs to be fixed."

"What's wrong with it?" Chloe asked.

"If you look at it, you'll find out," Pippa said unhelpfully. "Also, there's an issue with the header fonts. We do have a style guide, it has been provided to you. And yet, still, after six months of talking myself hoarse about the importance of continuity between our digital and print editions—nothing."

"Oh, I'm sorry," Chloe said. She didn't know why she was apologising. It certainly wasn't her fault. "I'll look into it."

"Well, while you're there, maybe you can figure out why the contact form boxes need to be so small. They are like a speck. I know we expect all of our readers to be young and perfectly abled but some of them need these." She pulled her glasses from the top of her head and waved them in Chloe's face.

If you need them, why are they on your head instead of your face? Chloe thought. But she wouldn't dare say anything. She was beginning to understand why she had been repeatedly warned by multiple people about Pippa.

"I'll… look into that as well."

"There are a lot of issues with the digital edition. But I think I'll wait and see your response on these before I waste my breath giving you the next batch of fixes." She turned on her heel and left.

Chloe let out a deep sigh and slowly turned back to her desk.

"The page flip is out of the box and can't be changed, the header is the same but displays slightly differently on the iPad, and the contact form is completely standard size," Natasha said.

Chloe frowned. "Then, why—"

"I have explained it all to her. Multiple times." Natasha looked up and met Chloe's eyes. "She doesn't *like* the page flip. Doesn't understand the difference in print and digital fonts. And doesn't wear her glasses."

"So, she thinks they are all fixes, but really they're…"

"Personal preferences," Natasha finished. "Exactly."

Chloe sagged into her chair. Dealing with Pippa wasn't going to be easy. In fact, it was going to be a lot more difficult than she thought. How did you fix things that weren't broken? She could already see her future: endlessly hearing complaints from Pippa about things that couldn't be fixed. Things that didn't need to be fixed.

So much for her sweeping into *Honey* and making everyone think she was amazing. She could just picture her probation meeting in three months. Pippa would be complaining that she approached her on her second day to fix a handful of issues and they were still not fixed. Helen would think about the times Chloe sat in meetings with nothing to say. Natasha wouldn't defend her. And then she'd have to pack her belongings into a cardboard box and leave the office.

She decided not to bring anything in to decorate her desk. Might as well make the box as light as possible.

She pulled her MacBook closer and stared blankly at the screen. If she wanted to keep this job, she needed to pull something out of the bag. She just didn't know what. Increasing the size of the contact form fields to something that could be seen from space might appease Pippa, temporarily, but it wasn't going to make much of a difference in the long run.

Her dad's face appeared in her mind. She smiled to herself. He'd just tell her to save the company, make a load of money, be voted Woman of the Year. Maybe run for prime minister, if the money was any good. No guidance on how to do any of that, just dogged assurance that she could.

She couldn't disappoint him. Not that he'd ever truly be disappointed in her, but she would feel like she let him down. She'd been talking for years about how amazing *Honey* was, and now she feared *Honey* wouldn't feel the same way about her.

An email came in from LinkedIn. Apparently twenty-eight of her connections were celebrating work anniversaries. The second she was told she got the job at *Honey*, she had updated her profile to show off her new place of employment. Now she wondered if that had been premature. LinkedIn was a great platform for telling the world how well you were doing by posting where you worked and what your job title was. It was also an easy way for people to see when you had failed.

She mainly used LinkedIn to connect with people who hadn't quite made the grade to be Facebook friends. They were people from school, university, and old work colleagues with whom she didn't want to lose touch. But they were also people who didn't need to see pictures of her drunk on her birthday or share their questionable political views.

Realisation started to dawn on her. She had a lot of LinkedIn contacts. Over two thousand. Every time she met someone in a business environment, she sent them a connection request. People usually said yes. LinkedIn was like a club where collecting contacts was the primary goal. Likewise, she never said no to a new connection request.

Surely one of her contacts might be able to help her. Business was all about connecting people. The right people, working together, could achieve magnificent things. Her marketing professor had said that repeatedly.

She opened LinkedIn and started to scroll through her newsfeed. She looked over birthdays, work anniversaries, news stories, internet memes. Maybe she was wrong. Maybe LinkedIn was a load of people who were bored at work and posting junk. It was like a work-acceptable Facebook.

She continued to scroll, wondering who half of the people even were.

Then she saw something of interest: a lesbian culture podcast. She'd vaguely heard of it, but she'd never really been one for podcasts. The person who had posted it was Donna Hayward, an old friend from university. She'd always suspected that Donna was gay, but she'd been too shy to ask. It seemed that Donna was the host of the show, *Girls About Town*.

The number of comments and likes were huge, well into the high tens of thousands.

Why have I never heard of this? Chloe wondered. *Because you uninstalled your podcast app to make room for that language app that you never use.*

She clicked on the podcast website and started to look around. A new show was put out every evening, and it was clear that the listenership was enormous.

This was it, this was what *Honey* needed. An opportunity to talk to their audience. She wondered if the podcast ran advertising slots. That would be the perfect way to get the *Honey* name out there.

She grabbed the contact email address from the website and went to her *Honey* inbox. She opened a new email. It was time to get back in touch with Donna Hayward.

CHAPTER SIXTEEN

THE MEETING HAD BEEN UNCOMFORTABLE. Fiona had done her best to remain stoically professional, but the same couldn't be said for Nicola, Rose, and Darcy. The three of them had laughed and joked the whole way through.

Fiona felt out of place, uninvited to the private jokes, and unwelcome. Deep down, she knew it wasn't entirely true. They had tried to bring her into the conversations, but each time she shot them down.

She knew it was jealousy, but she hated the way that Nicola was so sociable and could chat about anything with anyone. She wished she had that skill. Or half that skill. Even a quarter. Just enough to be able to speak with Nicola without feeling so damned inadequate and blurting out something ridiculous.

It had fallen to her several times to pull the meeting back on track. Which made her feel worse and worse about the stuck-in-the-mud image that she knew she was presenting.

Eventually, she'd had enough and decided to end the meeting. She couldn't stand being the fifth wheel any longer. She knew she had only herself to blame, but it didn't make it any easier.

"Right, well, I think that was a very productive meeting," she finished up. "Thank you for your time, Nicola. It's been very useful. As I say, I'm swamped today, but I'm sure we can talk more in the future."

She wasn't swamped, and she didn't want to talk more in the future. But it seemed like the right thing to say.

"No problem, glad to help." Nicola started to gather her belongings from the meeting room table.

Fiona's heart sunk as she watched Nicola prepare to leave. She didn't really want to end the meeting, she just wanted to be included in the chatter. Listening to Darcy and Rose incessantly gossiping and giggling with Nicola infuriated her. She wanted to be a part of it, but knew she couldn't. What she could do was end the meeting and pull them apart. To say she was busy and end the meeting had been a kneejerk reaction. One she was now regretting.

She wanted to spend more time with Nicola. She wanted to speak with her and actually demonstrate that she had something of worth to say. To prove that she wasn't all about work, that she actually had a social life and she could, when the occasion called for it, be faintly amusing.

But the in-jokes that she didn't quite grasp had got the better of her. A little voice inside reminded her that she'd know the details of the in-jokes if she actually spent time with them all. But she was so petrified that she'd make a fool of herself that she'd rather none of them spent any more time with Nicola.

"Wow," Nicola exclaimed as she looked at the clock on the wall. "Where does the time go? Say, do you girls want to go to lunch together? There's this new sushi place just up the road, cheap but really good?"

Fiona's eyes widened. Rose and Darcy looked like they wanted to go. She'd clearly talked herself out of an invite with her lie about being swamped with work. Ending the meeting early had ensured that she'd be pushed even further away from the socialising.

"Sure you can't join us?" Nicola asked her suddenly.

She swallowed and shook her head.

In an ideal world, she'd love to go. She'd make jokes, and everyone would laugh, and Nicola would see her for who she really was. But that never happened. Fiona made bad jokes, ones that made no sense. And everyone winced. It wasn't an ideal world.

"Unless you need one of them to woman the phones?" Nicola added. "I'm sorry, I shouldn't have randomly invited them without asking permission. I don't know what your setup is here, boss."

Fiona bristled slightly. Nicola had taken to calling her "boss."

"Nah, we have lunch together all the time," Rose interjected.

Fiona knew that she could *technically* say something to break up the lunchtime gathering. But Darcy and Rose looked excited, and she wasn't that mean.

"Rose is quite right. Enjoy your lunch." She picked up her notepad and fountain pen and breezed out of the room. She hoped that she gave the impression of someone who was busy and not someone who was in a strop, which was actually the case.

She threw her things down onto her desk. Flopping into the chair, she angrily shook the mouse to wake up her laptop. Staring at an unimportant email as if the future economy relied on it, she waited for the three women to grab their belongings and file out to lunch. Once they were out of sight, she let out a breath and closed her eyes.

"Where are they off to?" Lucy asked as she came back to her desk.

Fiona's eyes burst open. "A new sushi place. If you hurry, you can join them."

Lucy sat at her desk. "Too much to do, these ad spaces don't sell themselves. Sounds fun, why didn't you go?"

Fiona chuckled. "They don't want me there."

Lucy shrugged. "If you say so."

CHAPTER SEVENTEEN

IT WAS another scorching morning in London. Anyone who had been enjoying the prolonged heatwave was now nearing the end of their patience. London wasn't built for extreme heat. Or extreme cold. London was a Goldilocks sort of character that needed everything to be just right in order for it to function properly.

Most sensible people were now thoroughly over the idea of summer and looking forward to the cool breezes of autumn. And most sensible people were looking at Chloe like she was clinically insane.

Because Chloe emerged from the rotating doors into reception with a smile on her face and a spring in her step. While everyone else was exhausted from hot, sleepless nights and bracing themselves for yet more of the same, Chloe beamed as if she had won an all-expenses paid trip to the nearest walk-in freezer.

Chloe noticed the looks of bewilderment. She's seen them on the Tube, in the streets, and now in reception. She knew she looked insanely happy, but that was just because she was.

It was day three of her new job, and she'd learnt two things. Firstly, the smelly armpit people were also the people who ran late and therefore could be avoided by getting an earlier Tube. Secondly, London mornings were glorious.

She'd gotten off her train a couple of stops early and enjoyed a morning walk through Soho. Getting up earlier meant she had time to explore London and soak up some of the early morning sunshine.

After a little window shopping in Covent Garden, she'd walked towards the office. The spring in her step wasn't just because of the amazing weather and the thrill of working for *Honey*.

She'd spent an hour catching up with Donna Hayward the previous night, surprised to find out that she also lived in London. More surprised that she desperately wanted Chloe to come on the podcast to be interviewed about working at *Honey*.

Chloe had been unsure. She wasn't podcast material, she was boring and was on a low rung at the company. But Donna had been insistent. She even moved an interview with someone else for that evening, begging Chloe to come over for dinner and then to do the show.

The image of her dad smiling because she'd saved the world had appeared in her brain, and she was powerless to say no.

Of course, she had to do it. She could tell the tens of thousands of listeners about how amazing *Honey* was, how they had to pick up a copy immediately, and the magazine would be saved.

It was funny how life suddenly threw a curveball at you. One moment she was thinking that proving her worth to the company would be impossible, the next she really was in a situation to be able to save the company.

And so, she was happily smiling, annoying her fellow commuters. She even whistled as she stepped into the waiting elevator and selected the third floor.

She'd decided not to mention the interview, just in case something happened. She didn't want Pippa to elbow her way into the show instead, that would certainly spell the end of *Honey*. No, she'd decided to keep it quiet and then walk in on her fourth morning a superstar.

A hand caught the closing elevator door.

The doors opened, and Helen stepped in.

"Good morning," Helen greeted.

The whistle died on Chloe's lips.

"H-hi."

She felt flustered. The doors closed. She suddenly wondered if her morning walk had left her less than fresh. She was now trapped in a metal box with her boss. Her gorgeous boss.

"How are you settling in?" Helen asked.

"Great." Chloe grinned. She knew she looked like a psychopath, but she couldn't get her face to relax. She wished she wasn't so nervous around pretty women.

Say something else, anything, her mind implored her.

The elevator completed its short journey and the doors opened. They both stepped out and walked towards the office.

"Well, if you ever need anything, my door is always open," Helen said as they entered reception.

"Thanks. Mine, too," Chloe replied.

Helen smiled and made her way towards her office.

Chloe remained in the empty reception area until Helen was out of sight. The moment she'd gone, Chloe winced, bent forward and bit her fist.

Mine, too? MINE, TOO? She berated herself. *Of all the stupid replies…*

She stood tall and took a deep breath. She needed to get herself under control. Helen probably hadn't even heard what she said. Or had assumed that she'd misheard. If Chloe was lucky.

Her shoulders sagged. She trudged over to her desk and tossed her satchel underneath. She sat down and opened the lid of her laptop. She wondered if there was an online course for eradicating awkward behaviour. Maybe a self-help book entitled *How to Not Suck at Social Situations.*

Anxiety was common in Chloe's world. She became nervous in social situations and often said something ridiculous. But then she'd spend the next few hours dwelling on the fact. She hated it. It was like a double blow to her confidence.

"Morning," Kim said as she approached. She looked at Chloe with a frown. "Everything okay?"

"Yeah, just making Helen think I'm a moron." She sighed. Her good mood from the morning had faded.

Kim sat on the edge of her desk. "What happened?"

"She told me that her door was always open, you know, if I needed anything. So, I said, mine, too."

Kim snorted a laugh. "Whoops."

"Yeah. So now Helen thinks I'm an idiot."

"She doesn't," Kim reassured. "Helen's cool. And forget-ful, she won't remember that in ten minutes away."

"I hope not. I'll be remembering it enough for both of us." Chloe logged into her computer.

"You need to chill, it's no big deal. People say the wrong thing all the time. The world doesn't end." Kim smiled and shrugged her shoulders.

It was such an easy thing for someone to say. Someone who didn't suffer from anxiety. Just forget about it. It's no big deal. Move on.

Chloe couldn't be angry at Kim for being so blasé about it. Kim was easy-going and probably never worried about anything. She was laidback and seemed to be an expert in brushing things off. Chloe wished she'd inherited that from her family, but instead she had the ability to roll her tongue. Not as useful.

"I came over to tell you that Fridays are dress-down days around here. I figured Natasha wouldn't remember to tell you," Kim said.

"Oh, right, thanks for the heads-up." Chloe knew for certain that Natasha wouldn't tell her. So far, they had spoken strictly about work. She'd been offered minimal training and a stream of emails with tasks to complete. "How dress-down is it?"

"Whatever you like, just keep it clean. Me? I'll be getting my flip-flops out, it's too hot for these." She lifted her legs and tapped her black patent-leather brogues together.

"Not just flip-flops, I hope?" Chloe joked.

Kim laughed. "Maybe a pair of shorts and a tank. If I can be bothered."

Chloe wondered what she would wear. It was hard to gauge what the rest of the office would turn up in. She didn't want to look out of place. So far, everyone had been dressed fairly smartly. Wendy and Pippa were probably the most casual, everyone else wore varying degrees of casual business attire. Except Helen. Helen seemed to favour a power suit. Chloe couldn't complain about that.

"You worry a lot, don't you?" Kim asked.

Chloe nodded. "All the time."

"Wear whatever you like," Kim instructed. "And don't worry about Helen. She's totally forgotten that by now."

Chloe chuckled. Not worrying was easier said than done.

"I just don't want people to think I'm an idiot, you know? I really want to keep this job. The probation period is ticking away, and I feel like I have to live up to expectations."

"You've only worked here for three days," Kim reminded her.

"Every second counts," Chloe said.

"It will be fine. We all felt like we were useless when we first started. Then you slowly build up your confidence and you find your place in the company. I can't tell you how many important people I hung up on before I figured out how to transfer calls and not just cut them off." Kim laughed at the memory.

Chloe felt her heart palpitate at the very thought.

"If you're really worried about it," Kim continued, "then do something about it. Make yourself irreplaceable. Come up with an idea that, I don't know, saves us money. Then you'll definitely pass your probation."

"Well…" Chloe leaned forward as she whispered. "I do have one idea."

Kim looked around the quiet office to ensure they were alone. She leaned in. "Go on."

"An old friend of mine runs a lesbian culture podcast, *Girls about Town*? It's got a huge number of listeners. She wants me to go on there and talk about getting the job at *Honey* and working in digital and stuff. I think it's a great opportunity to let more people know about what a cool magazine it is."

"That sounds great," Kim said. "Have you let Fiona know?"

Chloe shook her head. "I'm kind of keeping it quiet. I want it to be me that does the interview. I'm worried that if I mention it to anyone else, then they'll want to do it. And it's my friend and I set it up, she wants to talk to me, so…"

"Yeah, I understand. Fiona would probably want to do it herself, and then it would be really dry. Or, worse, Pippa would catch wind of it and it would turn into a lecture about why no woman should ever feel obligated shave their legs."

Chloe shivered at the thought of Pippa's stern voice being broadcast to thousands of people. Listener figures would plummet. Phones would freeze.

"When are you doing it?" Kim asked.

"Tonight."

Kim blinked. "Wow, you don't hang around, do you?"

Chloe shook her head. "I told you about the door quote, yeah? I have to counteract that, fast!"

"Is it live?" Kim asked.

"No, they record it and then edit it and send it out. It will be up between eight and nine tonight."

"I'll definitely listen in! Lucy's over tonight for dinner so I can guarantee you will have two listeners already."

"But you already buy *Honey*," Chloe said.

Kim laughed. "No, we don't. We work here, we get a free copy."

Chloe rolled her eyes and playfully slapped Kim's arm. "You're a part of the problem."

CHAPTER EIGHTEEN

KIM HADN'T EXACTLY BEEN IGNORING Helen. She hadn't exactly been around either. But now she had to speak to her; she had to act like everything was normal. She stood up from her desk and knocked on the open door to Helen's office.

"Come in."

Kim took a step into the office. Helen's attention was focused on her monitor, her jaw clenched.

"Do you have a few minutes to go through your diary for the rest of the month?" Kim asked. It was clearly a bad time. Her heart thundered. Helen didn't get angry often, but she looked close now.

Helen gestured to the chair. "Close the door."

Kim closed the door and sat down. Helen hadn't taken her attention off her monitor. Kim wondered if she was reading the email from Christine. But then again, it was only a couple of lines, she'd be done by now.

Her heart started to race at the mere thought of the

email and her betrayal of Helen's trust in reading it. She was useless at lying, she imagined she practically had it written on her face.

"Have you looked at my inbox lately?" Helen inquired. She sat back in her chair and pinned Kim with a sad expression.

"Nope," Kim said quickly. Then she thought she better make an effort of looking like she had at least considered the question. She frowned, as if trying to remember. "Nope," she repeated, "not for a while, at least."

Helen slowly nodded. Her eyes drifted back to her monitor.

Kim wondered if there was some digital footprint she was unaware of. Maybe Helen knew that she had opened the email. Maybe there was some system that accessed the webcam and took a picture of people snooping. She'd seen people posting pictures online of pets trying to unlock smartphones and setting off the camera in the process. Was Helen looking at a photo of Kim spying on her emails?

Her heartbeat was now going into overdrive, and she wondered if she might pass out.

"My ex wants the house," Helen finally said. "My house."

Kim sucked a breath into sore lungs. "Oh?"

"I bought that house before I met her. But, because she set up a business in the old outbuilding, which, by the way, I paid through the nose to convert into a workspace for her, she now wants the house. Not just the outbuilding, the house."

Helen reached forward and slammed the lid of her laptop closed.

"To be honest," Helen continued, "if there were no monetary loss involved, I'd do it. I'm positive she slept with her high schooler in our bed. God knows what they did and where in that house. I saw a fingerprint on the window the other week, and I wondered if it was hers... the high schooler."

"She's not actually a high schooler, is she?" Kim asked.

The topic of Helen's separation and then divorce was spoken about often, but the new woman on the scene was simply referred to as "the high schooler." Kim knew nothing about her, other than the fact she was, presumably, very young.

"Nineteen," Helen replied sourly.

Kim let out a low whistle. "That's young."

"They met in a coffee shop in some trendy part of Shoreditch. High School smelt money and desperation, I suppose." Helen shook her head and leaned forward. "Love doesn't always last, Kim. I never thought I'd get divorced. If we ever split, I assumed we'd talk amicably and like sensible adults who cared about each other. Now I'm fighting for everything I have, everything I built up in my life. Because my ex is dating a high schooler and my ex-father-in-law is a lawyer who never liked me."

Kim wished she could say something to make Helen feel better, but she knew there was nothing to be said. Helen was a nice person who was being stabbed in the back by her ex-wife. There weren't words that could fix that.

"Do you want me to hire a hitman?" Kim joked.

Helen smirked. "No. Don't deny me the pleasure of doing it myself!" She chuckled bitterly. "Anyway, you're not here to hear about my woes. Did you need something?"

Kim waved her iPad. "Your diary for the rest of the month."

Helen nodded and looked through the papers on her desk for her leather journal. Kim's heart bled for her boss.

Helen unearthed her journal. She put her glasses on and started flipping through pages to find the correct day.

Kim felt the pit of guilt in her stomach starting to grow. She didn't know how much longer she could keep the truth from Helen.

CHAPTER NINETEEN

FIONA SUNK into a leather chair in the ground floor's reception to try to catch her breath. It was ridiculously hot outside. She'd be pleased when summer had a break. A storm would be nice about now. Some rain. Anything to stop the relentless heat.

She closed her eyes and sucked in a few breaths of air conditioning.

Beads of sweat gathered on her forehead, clumping her hair to her face. She reached up an hand and tried to sweep her hair back. She dabbed at her forehead with a tissue. She imagined that she looked a mess, but she didn't care. All that mattered now was taking a few moments' respite from the heat.

Honey wasn't the plushest office she'd ever worked in, but they always had heat in the winter and cool air in the summer.

The meeting she'd just attended at one of London's leading advertising agencies had been horrendous. The air conditioning had broken. Everyone was grouchy, sweating, and exhausted. Then she'd had to get the Tube back to the office in much the same conditions. The walk from the station to the office was short, but it was also in direct sight of the midday sun.

Just before she entered the building, her vision had started to blur, and she briefly wondered if she was going to pass out. Mercifully, the seats in reception saved any potential embarrassment. Though, she still felt like death.

A nice, cold glass of water, she thought. *That will help.*

She dragged herself up from her seat and walked over to the elevators. In hindsight, it would have been wise to stop on the way back to the office and get a drink. The queues out of the door of the first two places she saw put pay to that idea.

Soho was a tourist trap, especially in summer months. The idea of getting lunch from the local sandwich shop in hot weather was not worth thinking about.

She entered the elevator and selected the third floor. Thankful to have the car to herself, she leaned against the wall and waved her hand over her face. The air conditioning was welcome, but she still felt like she was suffocating. The doors opened, she stepped out of the elevator.

As she approached the kitchen, she heard a familiar voice.

Nicola.

She toyed with her necklace nervously. She hadn't expected Nicola to be in the office. Or, more accurately, in the kitchen. Where she needed to go to grab a glass of water.

Peals of laughter fell from the kitchen. Fiona leaned

against the wall and cursed her luck. She walked a little closer, careful to remain out of sight.

There were two voices. One was unmistakably Nicola, the other was unfamiliar.

She took a breath to steel herself and walked into the kitchen. She went straight to the cabinet and pulled out a mug, then glanced at the table in the corner of the room.

The new girl, Chloe, and Nicola sat next to each other, looking at a number of printed photographs strewn across the table.

What has she got to do with photography? Fiona groused to herself. *It's completely out of her remit.*

She filled her mug with water from the cooler and took the opportunity to eavesdrop.

"I just think I got the lighting all wrong here," Chloe said.

"Yeah, you did. The first thing you need to remember when lining up any shot is the lighting. Is it natural? Artificial? Where is it coming from? How much light is there? Once you work with light, and don't ignore it, you'll find your photography will improve."

"Oh, I don't think so," Chloe said. "I think it's more than just lighting issues. Look at these prints if you want proof!"

Nicola chuckled. "Well, yeah, but I think you deliberately picked out some of the worst so we could laugh about them. See, this one, this one is okay."

"I've always liked that one. I have a larger print in my bedroom."

Fiona sipped her water.

She kept her back to them. Her temper was growing as

she listened to their chatter. Why was Chloe even speaking to Nicola? Why was she wasting her time, trying to get professional insight into her apparently atrocious skills? And why did the young blonde feel the need to mention her bedroom? It was all completely inappropriate.

She spun around. "Chloe, I think you're wasting Nicola's valuable time. She has better things to be doing than helping you change careers. And I'm sure you have work to be doing."

Chloe's face fell. "She said it was okay. And it's my lunchtime."

Fiona glared at her. She couldn't believe the girl was answering her back. Making her look like a fool when she was clearly in the wrong and Fiona was clearly in the right.

She approached the table and slammed her mug down.

"Nicola is a professional. She doesn't need to be wasting her time looking at this… this rubbish. Of course, she said yes, she's a kind person. But you're taking advantage of that kind nature with this…" She picked up the first photograph she saw.

"Anyone can see that this is awful. You don't need a professional's opinion to see that this is shocking. The framing, the lighting. It's abysmal. Anyone with eyes can see that. You don't need a professional to tell you the obvious."

Nicola stood up and snatched the photo out of her hand.

"Actually, that's one of mine," she said. "And I offered to help Chloe because I'm interested in nurturing talent. Which she has bags of. And she doesn't deserve to be spoken to like that, and neither do I." She shook her head as she stared Fiona down. "Wow, I had you all wrong."

Fiona's eyes widened. She had no idea where her outburst had come from. She wondered if it was the heat. And the insane jealousy that had settled on her like a heavy cloud.

Nicola had already gathered her belongings and was heading towards the door.

"I'll catch you later, Chloe," she said as she left.

Fiona covered her mouth with her hand. She couldn't believe what had just happened. Why did she always do this? What was wrong with her?

Chloe was quickly packing her things away, eager to escape as well.

"Chloe, I am so sorry," Fiona said sincerely. "I honestly have no idea what just came over me. I've been in a two-hour meeting with no air conditioning and then the Tube broke down and… there's no excuse. I'm sorry, that was inexcusable."

"It's fine," Chloe said. She was still anxiously sweeping up her photographs and placing them in a folder. It was clearly not fine. Fiona knew that Chloe was just saying whatever she could to stop the mad woman talking and get out of her way.

She couldn't believe her reaction. And to speak to a colleague in that tone was unbelievable. Especially a new, young member of the team. She had to fix it.

"It's not," Fiona said firmly. "I'm truly, very sorry. I should never have spoken to you like that."

Chloe paused. Her eyes slowly looked up at Fiona's. She'd obviously not been expecting a heartfelt apology and was now analysing the intent behind it.

"It's okay," she said, with a little more feeling this time.

"I know what you mean about the heat, it's really bad today. I feel a little tetchy, too."

Fiona let out a sigh of relief. "Absolutely. I'm not usually like that, I really don't know what came over me."

Chloe visibly relaxed, the tension in her body slipping away. She smiled.

"Don't worry about it," she said.

"I do," Fiona admitted. "I feel terrible." She looked at her watch and then at Chloe. "Do you have anything particular you need to do within the next, say, hour or so?"

Chloe shook her head.

"Shall we get out of here, and I'll buy you a drink? My apology. We can talk about the new email templates, but over a nice mocktail or glass of wine. If you want to, of course. I just want to apologise and prove I'm not a complete lunatic. I'll message Natasha and tell her where you are."

Chloe's eyes lit up. "That sounds great. I'd love to get out of the office for a while."

"Me, too," Fiona said. "Meet you downstairs in five?"

CHAPTER TWENTY

KIM'S FINGERS paused over the keyboard. She looked up and saw Fiona and Chloe walking back into the office.

"Oh boy," she muttered to herself.

She turned her chair and looked through the door to Helen's office. The editor had looked up from her laptop and was staring as the women crossed the office. Her eyes flitted to Kim's. She quirked her head, silently ordering an immediate meeting with Fiona.

Kim jumped up from her desk and hurried across the office. Before Fiona had a chance to sit down, she approached her with an apologetic look.

"Helen would like to see you."

"Now?" Fiona asked.

Kim nodded.

Fiona raised an eyebrow. "Is there a problem?"

"Helen will tell you." Kim wasn't about to get involved.

Fiona let out a sigh. She put her bag on the floor by her desk and gestured for Kim to lead the way. Kim turned and walked back to her desk, sensing Fiona's presence behind her. She paused by Helen's door and gestured for Fiona to go inside.

"Kim, can you come in here as well, please?" Helen asked.

Damn. She'd been so close to escaping. She walked into the office and took a seat next to Fiona. Fiona looked from Kim to Helen with confusion. Clearly, she had no idea what had happened during her absence.

"Everything okay?" she asked.

"Nicola came in earlier," Helen said, almost conversationally. "She told me that she isn't interested in working with *Honey* for the foreseeable future."

"Oh," Fiona replied.

"She suggested that you might know something about that?" Helen continued.

Kim couldn't help but look at Fiona. She was curious to know what had gone on. She liked Fiona. She was nice, professional, and even funny when she wanted to be. But there was something about her relationship with Nicola. Nicola got on with everyone, except Fiona. There was some weird kind of energy there that Kim couldn't quite place.

"Well—" Fiona began. Her cheeks were starting to blush and she played with her necklace.

"Do you know why we use Nicola as our primary freelance photographer?" Helen interrupted.

"Because she's the best?" Fiona asked.

Helen barked a laugh. "No. She's not the best. Don't get me wrong, she's very good, but she's not the *best*. The reason we use her is because she is very cheap. She's bisexual, and her personal goals align with the magazine. She wants to see

Honey do well, and so she provides us with an enormous discount on her work."

"Oh," Fiona said again.

"Have you ever seen a magazine without photography, Fiona?" Helen asked casually.

"No—"

"Page after page of text," Helen continued. "Like a newspaper from the turn of the century. The previous century."

"No."

"Kim, have you seen a magazine without photography?"

"No," Kim replied.

Kim had never been more thankful to be on Helen's side and not in Fiona's seat. Suddenly the idea of coming clean about reading Christine's email seemed like a very bad one.

"Kim's not seen a magazine without photography either," Helen said. "Would you like *Honey* to create a new trend? The only magazine without a single... sodding... photograph?"

"No, of course—"

"Good. Whatever you broke, however you broke it, now is time for you to fix it," Helen ordered.

Fiona's jaw dropped open. She looked from Helen to Kim and then back again.

"But—"

"Fix it," Helen repeated.

Fiona hurried from the office. Kim wished she could do the same, but she had clearly been called in for a reason.

Helen angrily shuffled some pieces of paper.

"We need to see if we can find another photographer," Helen said. "But I don't know where we'll find the budget."

"You really think Nicola won't come back?" Kim asked.

"She was very angry. She might cool down, who knows? I can't wait around to find out, we need to have a backup plan. We need a new photographer to deal with next month's shoot, and then we need to look at stock photography websites to plug the rest of the gap."

"Did she say what Fiona had said?"

"No. Just to ask Fiona. Which I'd rather not do, as I have a hundred other things that require my attention. I'll give Fiona the chance to fix it, and if she can't then I'll attempt to mediate. But we need a Plan B in the meantime."

Helen tried to sign a piece of paper, but the Biro she was using didn't work. She sighed and threw it into the bin. She plucked another pen out of the pot on her desk.

"Maybe I'll have a week where all hell doesn't break loose sometime soon," she muttered under her breath.

CHAPTER TWENTY-ONE

CHLOE RAN UP THE STAIRS, two at a time. She arrived on the platform at exactly the same moment that the train started to leave.

"Damn," she muttered.

She panted for breath and held onto the nearby pillar to steady herself.

After a moment, she stood up and looked at the screen to see when the next train would arrive. She had a twenty-minute wait.

A small coffee shop on the platform beckoned her.

She'd left the office late due to Pippa's insistence that she look at another non-issue with the digital edition. She couldn't tell her that she had to leave to conduct an interview and so she'd had to sit patiently and listen to Pippa tell her why digital was a farce, her leg twitching as she watched the minutes go by. Finally, Pippa had ran out of steam and gone to complain about other things to someone else, allowing Chloe to rush out of the office.

Now, she was late. And hungry.

The moment she left the office, she'd texted Donna to let her know that she was running late. A few texts back and forth, and they had decided that Chloe would eat on the way and still conduct the interview that evening as planned. Otherwise the interview would be delayed by up to three weeks because of scheduling.

Chloe couldn't wait three weeks, she needed to prove her worth as soon as possible. Not to mention the fact that she had spent the entire day worrying about the interview. Would she have anything interesting to say? Would she freeze up? Would her voice sound strange? No one liked to hear the sound of their own voice, but was Chloe's unusually abnormal? She couldn't spend the next three weeks worrying about such things. It was best to get it done and out of the way.

She entered the coffee shop and stood in front of the refrigerated unit, staring at the end-of-the-day array of sandwiches, wraps, and baguettes. She leaned in closer, pretending to look at something but actually just enjoying the feel of cool air on her face.

The atmosphere at *Honey* that day had been as thick as the humidity outside. Something had clearly happened that had gone over her head. Helen was fuming about something. Kim was keeping her head down. Everyone in marketing was silent as the grave. Fiona, who had been laughing and joking over mocktails at the downstairs bar, had become very agitated and quiet after a meeting with Helen.

Chloe didn't feel she could ask what was going on, so she just got on with her work. Tess had made a coffee run late in the afternoon and had given Chloe a comforting squeeze on the shoulder as she placed a cup of tea on her desk. If tactile gestures could speak, this one would say, *I know, don't worry, this will pass.*

But she couldn't help but worry. Something had happened. It had thrown the mood of the office off. She suspected it was something to do with the financial issues that everyone was trying, and failing, to not mention.

Her phone buzzed in her pocket. She pulled it out and looked at the screen. It was her parents.

She put her headphones in and swiped to answer the call.

"Hey," she greeted.

"Hello." Dad sounded chipper. "We have you on loud-speaker."

This was a relatively new development. After years of Chloe spending an hour on the phone to one parent, to then be handed over and spend another hour speaking to the other, they had worked out a better system.

"Hello!" Mum said, her voice loud and clear as if she were calling space.

"Hey, Mum." She grabbed a sandwich and a bottle of water and walked over to the bored employee. "Everything okay with you two?"

"Yes," Dad said. "We didn't get a chance to arrange our next meet-up. You left so fast…"

It had been intentional. At the end of every family get-together was the half-hour discussion about when they would see each other again. As if all parties had travelled from distant lands. In reality, they all lived within a twenty-minute car journey of each other, but her parents had an obsession with getting something in the calendar.

"I had an early start the next morning," Chloe defended herself. She looked apologetically at the server, she hated being on her phone when paying for something. The server didn't even make eye contact. Instead she scanned the sandwich as if it had personally offended her family.

"What are you doing this weekend?" Dad asked.

Sleeping, Chloe thought. "I'm not sure…"

"You could come over for lunch," Mum added.

The eagerness to quiz her about work and potential matches was palpable. They had seen first-hand how devastated she had been after the breakup. For some reason they both believed that getting into another relationship would be the cure.

"Can I call you nearer the time? I think I might have something on, but I don't have my diary with me."

"Either day is fine," Dad said.

Trapped. They weren't going to let her go. She was definitely seeing them at the weekend.

"Okay. Yeah, sounds good." She paid for her sandwich and drink.

"So, how is everything?" Mum asked.

Chloe closed her eyes for a moment, wishing for strength she didn't feel. She'd just started a new job, she was exhausted. Surely, they could give her a little respite before grilling her? Then she remembered, they'd both retired and had nothing to do but snoop into other people's lives. Neither of them had hobbies, preferring to live vicariously through her and Kevin. And Kevin never had anything out of the ordinary going on. He worked the same job, had the same girlfriend, had no intention of marriage or kids. Any interesting gossip was sure to come from Chloe and not him.

Besides, she was the one who'd failed so spectacularly that she had to run home to Mum and Dad. At the moment they were focused on her with laser precision.

"Yeah, good." She picked up her items and walked over to a table. "I'm just in a café, so I'm eating a sandwich."

"For dinner?" Mum wasn't impressed. In her world, dinner was hot food, with cutlery, at a table.

"Yeah, I had to stay late and then I have this thing after work so… you know, I have to go." She knew it was pointless. They wouldn't let her go.

"What thing?" Dad asked, not getting the hint.

"A… podcast." Chloe winced the moment she said the word. She knew what was coming.

"What's a podcast?" Dad asked.

"It's like Internet radio," she explained.

"You're on the radio? How do we listen to that?" he asked.

Chloe really didn't have time to explain to her parents, who had just mastered the art of loudspeaker, the apps they could install and searches they would need to perform in order to listen to a lesbian podcast which would frankly go over their heads.

"I'll… show you at the weekend," she said. Fate sealed. She'd have to go now.

"What will you be talking about?" Mum asked.

"The magazine, talking about what they do and what I do."

"P-O-D-C-A-S-T," Dad said slowly, obviously typing it

into his iPad. "Okay, Wikipedia… iTunes… what do I need to click?"

He was oblivious to the fact that Chloe just wanted to eat her sandwich in peace and get to the recording. He was now a man on a mission.

"Can I show you at the weekend?" she asked. She opened her sandwich and prepared to take a bite.

"Set up an account," Dad read aloud.

Chloe winced. She had no idea what account he was trying to set up.

"It's a bit late for a radio show," Mum said. "And right during dinner time." She hadn't gotten over the sandwich for dinner tragedy.

"Well, I don't have any other time to do it," Chloe hinted. "I'm really busy with work, and then… you know, I'm tired after work. As I just started."

"Can't you do it *at* work? It is *for* work, after all," Mum said. "It's silly that they want you to do it now."

"Well, it's not really for work, as such. It's more about me. And I didn't really want work to know about it. Not until I'd done it."

"Why not?" Mum asked.

Chloe lowered her carb-heavy meal. She clearly wasn't going to get off the phone any time soon.

"Because I wanted to be the one to do it, it's a friend who runs the podcast and I set up the interview myself. I was worried that if I mentioned it, they'd send someone else."

"Do you get paid overtime?" Mum quizzed.

"They want a password, what's my password?" Dad asked.

CHAPTER TWENTY-TWO

DARCY HAD FOUND the perfect spot. The large room had five doors leading to other rooms in the National Gallery. She stood in the exact location where she could easily see all doorways, and more importantly, could be seen from them.

Now it was a matter of waiting. Something she wasn't good at. The more time that passed, the more nervous she became.

The programme of events for the evening was tucked under her crossed arms. Holding it in her hand made her shaking too obvious. She was trying to look lost in thought, staring at the same oil painting as if it was speaking to her on some deep level.

In truth, she hadn't given it more than two seconds of her time. While her eyes were focused forward, all her senses were on edge. She listened to the people around her, hoping to detect Celia's silky tones.

So far, nothing. It had been over an hour, and her legs were beginning to ache. She hadn't listened to the talk.

Ironically, she was terrified of seeing Celia in the room. In her mind, she had a plan and she wanted to stick with it. Everyone who went into the talk then walked around the gallery to look at the pieces on display. It was her hope that Celia would enter the room and see Darcy *first*.

Of course, Darcy would see her as well. But she'd pretend that she hadn't. She'd be casually examining a piece of art, distracted from the world around her. Looking like she just happened to be there and wasn't, effectively, stalking someone.

Celia would be surprised, impressed even. She'd approach Darcy in an out-of-work setting and Darcy would finally be able to speak to her. To recite her rehearsed lines and make Celia understand how much they had in common. It was step one in a series of steps, but it was the most important one.

The only problem was that Celia was nowhere in sight.

Sweat had formed along her hairline. She wondered what she looked like to outsiders. Were other people looking at her and wondering what was so fascinating about the piece? Did they think she was having a stroke? *Was* she having a stroke?

She took a deep breath to try to keep herself calm. No easy task. As the minutes ticked by, her anxiety levels had gone through the roof. Her eyes flicked to one of the doorways, a large crowd of people was gathering in the next room.

Then she saw her. Celia was in the crowd, laughing, a glass of champagne in her hand. Celia was always impeccably dressed. Tonight, she wore a long cream skirt and heels, a high-necked white lace top and a knee-length cream-and-white jacket. Her shoulder-length light brown hair was perfectly straight and tucked behind her ears.

Darcy quickly looked away. She couldn't be seen staring. She couldn't be seen seeing her at all. Her whole plan was based on appearing as if she had no idea Celia was at the event.

An attack of nerves caused her body to shake. She shifted her balance a little, trying to pretend it was a cramp and not unbridled fear.

She stared intently at the painting. The sweat under her hair began dripping down her back. She took a steady breath, reminding herself to breathe evenly and calmly.

Doubt crept in.

Maybe this was the wrong idea. Maybe Celia wouldn't recognise her. Perhaps she'd say the wrong thing and alienate her forever. Was the painting one she didn't like? How would Darcy even know?

The group entered the room.

Her breath caught in her throat, and she wondered if she was about to pass out. She couldn't help but quickly glance at the new arrivals. She frowned. Celia wasn't with them. But these were definitely the people she'd been talking to.

Darcy took a step to the side, looking around the chattering mass. Celia remained in the other room, being helped into her coat by a member of staff.

She's leaving, Darcy realised. Her heart thundered in her chest. All her planning had gone out of the window. The preparation, the rehearsing in front of the mirror, all a waste of time.

If she were braver, she would cross the room and say

hello. Comment at how she was just about to leave herself and how funny it was they were both at the same event. They'd walk to the door together, exchange a few words.

But she wasn't that brave. Just thinking about it made her sick to her stomach. She wanted to talk to Celia, it just had to be in a way she had prepared for. The stakes were too high to wing it.

She turned around and quickly crossed the room, eager to put some distance between them. She'd been standing in one spot for so long that her legs had gone to sleep, and she stumbled a little.

Since she had arrived, she'd remained in the same position, eager that she didn't accidentally run into Celia and ruin her planning. Now she knew exactly where she was, and she was able to hurry in the opposite direction.

She kept moving through room after room, grateful for her knowledge of the gallery and all its exits. She brushed past the doorman of the west wing exit and rushed down the stone steps.

She stopped at the bottom of the stairs and sucked in a deep breath. Her heart was racing. She chided herself for not being adult enough to be able to just approach the woman of her dreams.

A couple of tears came loose from her waterlogged eyes. She walked away from the gallery, thankful for the late hour and the darkness that shielded her face.

As always, London was busy. She navigated her way through the crowds, heading towards the river. Walking along the Thames always calmed her. Hopefully the serene waters would help put the evening's events behind her.

She looked at her phone to check the time. She

scrubbed away a few notifications before seeing one that caught her eyes. *The Girls About Town* podcast had an interview with… Chloe Dixon?

Intrigued, she got her headphones out and tuned into the show.

CHAPTER TWENTY-THREE

Kᴉᴍ ᴘᴏᴜʀᴇᴅ two glasses of red wine. It was the cheap stuff, but her stomach had developed a resistance to it.

Lucy carried the dirty plates into the kitchen.

"You didn't have to do that," Kim said.

"I wanted to. You cooked." Lucy opened the dishwasher and pulled the wire rack out.

"No, no," Kim insisted. "I'll do that. Here." She handed over a glass of wine.

Lucy took the glass and smirked. "Are you one of those people who doesn't like other people stacking the dishwasher? One of those people who restack things?"

Kim poked her tongue out. She started to stack the dishwasher, admittedly in the way she liked it. So, maybe she had restacked the dishwasher in the past. But she knew that the top right-hand corner just didn't get things clean. That wasn't being picky, that was knowing her appliances and their quirks.

"Oh my god, you are," Lucy chuckled.

"I don't say anything, and you immediately think I'm guilty?" Kim asked.

"Yep. Your silence condemned you." Lucy leaned on the counter, obviously watching Kim bend down and fill the dishwasher.

"Enjoying the view?" Kim put an extra sway into her movements.

"A lot. Seriously, though, thank you for inviting me over. And cooking, it's really helped to take my mind off things."

"How is the job hunt going?" Kim hated that Lucy would be leaving the office. Some people might have wanted a little space from their partner, but Kim didn't think she would survive not seeing her girlfriend every day. She'd always loved her job, but now she was thinking of leaving as well. Escape the potential job cuts. And the memories. And Helen's wrath.

"It's slow. There isn't a lot in the market at the moment," Lucy admitted. "I've sorted my CV out and sent it to a million people. I sorted out my LinkedIn profile, too."

"I saw your new profile pic. Looking good, Miss Bryce." Kim stood up and closed the dishwasher door with her foot. "So, nothing much happening at the moment?"

"No. I expected some phone calls today, you know, recruitment consultants asking me to repeat what my CV already says… but nothing."

Kim could tell that Lucy was starting to worry. She'd already admitted that she had no savings, no safety net.

"Maybe things will pick up at *Honey*?" Kim said. "Your new campaign is doing well, you mentioned?"

Lucy's face brightened a little. "Yeah. I've got a few new

advertisers on the hook at a higher price. I suppose it depends on how quickly Helen will move on Christine's advice. And how quickly *Honey* figures go up… or down."

"Let's hope for up," Kim said. She always believed that a positive attitude yielded results.

"I don't see what's going to change without more budget," Lucy admitted. "We need to advertise… a lot. But there's no money for that. Rose is good at social media, but I can't see her starting a massive trend for *Honey* in the next few days."

Kim glanced up at the kitchen clock. "There's always the *Girls About Town* podcast."

Lucy looked confused.

"Oh! I forgot to tell you." Kim smacked her forehead with the palm of her hand. "Chloe is on the podcast tonight. She's going to talk about *Honey* and try to get more people to buy copies."

Lucy's eyes shone with enthusiasm. "That's a great idea, how did she swing that?"

"Her old university friend runs the podcast."

"They have a massive fanbase, if we can tap that then… when's it on? Tonight?"

Kim smiled, it was so nice to see Lucy light up. "Yeah, shall we listen in the living room? It should be live by now."

"Sure."

They quickly got settled on the sofa. Wine glasses on the coffee table, window open to let a light breeze through the small apartment. Kim pushed some buttons on her iPhone, eventually finding the show and cranking up the volume.

They listened to a few minutes of chatter and introduction from the host, Donna, before Lucy let out a sigh.

"Can we fast forward to Chloe?"

Kim ran her finger along the screen, pausing every few moments to listen in. Suddenly she heard a familiar voice and lifted her finger.

"… and that's why I always loved *Honey* when I was a teenager," Chloe said.

Lucy squeezed Kim's arm. Kim leaned into their embrace and listened.

"But, you were saying that *Honey* doesn't have the readership it used to have?" Donna asked.

"No, it's a real shame. But I'm hoping that speaking with you and getting the word out there will make people more aware that *Honey* is available and how great it is."

"Would you say *Honey* is in trouble?"

There was a moment of silence. Lucy's fingers dug into Kim's arm nervously.

"Well…" Chloe eventually spoke up. "All magazines are experiencing a drop in sales. With so much content available online for free—"

"People aren't willing to pay for magazines," Donna interrupted. "That's presumably had a big effect on *Honey Magazine*, an already niche product. I can't imagine it was making much money to start with… and now with a lower circulation… things must be tight?"

"Um, well, not tight exactly. I mean, no one is wasting money. The magazine is a really well-made product—"

"Just one that isn't selling well?"

"Well… um…" Chloe said.

"Shit," Lucy mumbled. She paused the show. "She's making it sound like we're in trouble."

"That's good, isn't it? Rally people to buy?" Kim asked.

"No, it's bad. Advertisers don't like magazines that don't sell. Or magazines in financial trouble, ones that might go bust. This isn't an interview about Chloe's work at *Honey*, this is about Donna getting the inside track on what's happening at *Honey*, getting a scoop that we're in trouble."

"But if people think we're in trouble, they'll buy more copies, surely?" Kim asked.

"Only if there are copies to buy. If advertisers leave and money dries up, we won't be able to put out an edition for people to buy." Lucy shook her head. "And this host has it in for us."

"The host is goading her," Kim agreed.

"Has Chloe had media training? Why is she doing this show on behalf of the company? Does Helen know?" Lucy asked. She got to her feet, snatched up her wine glass, and walked over to the window to get some air.

Kim was starting to see that keeping Chloe's secret was a big mistake. She should have told Helen, or at least told Chloe to tell Helen.

"No one knows, she wanted it to be a surprise," Kim admitted.

"'Surprise, I've told everyone you're about to go under and all your advertisers will run for the hills,'" Lucy mocked. She turned from the window and gestured towards the phone. "Turn it back on, maybe it gets better."

Kim unpaused the show.

"You heard it here first, folks," Donna said. "*Honey* magazine is struggling, let's do what we can to help."

She paused the show again.

Lucy leaned her head on the window frame and sighed. "We're fucked."

CHAPTER TWENTY-FOUR

WHILE THE LONDON Underground was a technical marvel and exceled at transporting large numbers of people around the city quickly, they still had a way to go when it came to braking.

Fiona sat in the middle of the row of seats. While she was glad to have a seat, she wasn't glad that the driver was clearly fresh out of training. As they approached stations, the brakes were harshly slammed on and everyone pitched forward. When they left, they sped up so quickly that passengers leaned in the opposite direction.

She tried to anticipate the movements, but often failed and ended up hurtling into the person beside her. Who fell into the person beside them, and so on. They were human dominoes.

Usually Fiona would have found this intolerable and would be huffing in annoyance. But she was too focused on her phone. She stared at the two words she had managed to come up with.

Dear Nicola

It wasn't a great start. But considering calling the woman had proved fruitless and that Fiona wasn't about to try to grovel on a voicemail, this was all she had.

She'd been working on her typed apology the previous night and throughout the morning. She'd written plenty of options. But they all ended up being deleted. No matter what she wrote, it seemed to come out wrong.

Often it turned into a sarcastic sort of non-apology. She just couldn't understand why she did it. Why did communicating with Nicola always bring out the worst in her? Why couldn't she just act like a normal person?

She started to type again.

Following the unfortunate episode yesterday…

Too formal.

The train screeched to a halt, and she fell into her neighbour.

"Sorry," she muttered.

The person on the other side of her mumbled a half-felt apology.

She slowly deleted each letter of the sentence.

Fiona blew out a breath and looked up. Everyone looked stressed. The heatwave continued and being underground at eight in the morning with hardly any oxygen wasn't where anyone wanted to be.

At least she should be grateful for Wi-Fi. It was a relatively new and welcome addition to her commute. Previously, people had been forced to read books or play Candy Crush. Now they all had their noses buried in their phones, presumably dealing with emails.

She knew that she probably had an inbox of over a hundred messages that could really do with her attention. Unlike previous mornings, she hadn't even looked at them. She knew that this one was the most important. Not just because Helen would murder her if she didn't fix it, but because she knew she had overreacted. She had shown the worst of herself. Because she was stressed, overheated... and jealous.

She looked at the screen again. Words often failed her when it came to Nicola, but the moment she was on her own she often felt the same thing. That she had acted foolishly. And that she wanted to apologise for it.

Maybe it wasn't about creating the perfect excuse for her unacceptable behaviour. Maybe it was time to say what she really felt.

I'm sorry. I'm an idiot. I can't seem to act like a human being around you. I apologise from the bottom of my heart for being a rude, inconsiderate arse.

She hit send and let out a deep sigh.

It probably wasn't going to solve anything, but at least she had finally said what she had been thinking for months.

CHAPTER TWENTY-FIVE

Darcy loitered in reception. It had to be her. Rose was running late, and Kim was talking Helen down from a murderous rampage.

While she usually didn't enjoy work drama, this particular incident was timely. It meant that her utter failure to bump into Celia the previous evening wasn't going to be the topic of discussion. Not for a while anyway.

She'd never actively hope for someone else's day to come crashing down in flames, but she'd certainly take advantage of the opportunity to move the subject away from her.

Fiona breezed into the office. She paused only upon seeing Darcy in reception and raised her eyebrow in a silent question.

"Just waiting for someone," Darcy said, suitably vaguely.

It was true. She was waiting for Chloe. Waiting to warn her that all hell was about to break loose. But she didn't want to tell Fiona that. Fiona probably wouldn't approve of Chloe being given any such warning.

Luckily, it looked like Fiona was unaware of what had transpired the night before. Sadly, that ignorance wouldn't last long. It looked like it might be another tense day at the *Honey* office.

Fiona nodded and walked towards the inner office. Darcy looked at her watch. There was another half an hour until the workday technically started. She hoped that Chloe would arrive soon.

"Blithering idiot!"

Darcy jumped. She turned around to see Pippa almost take the door off its hinges in her hurry to enter the office.

"Where is she?" Pippa demanded. "Or has she seen sense and decided to not come back?"

Darcy stood tall. "Who?" she asked innocently.

Pippa narrowed her eyes, trying to ascertain if Darcy knew what she was talking about.

"New girl," Pippa spat out.

At least she hasn't learnt her name yet, Darcy thought. *Less chance of a murder at Chloe's personal address.*

"Not seen her."

"Well, when you do, tell her that I want to see her. Preferably, her head on a spike! I see Helen has put together a statement, fat lot of good that will do! No one reads the bloody things anyway." Pippa stormed into the inner office.

Any chance of a quiet day at *Honey* had now been well and truly blown out of the water. In a few minutes, Fiona would be aware of the situation. Open-plan offices were nice and bright and easy to navigate, but news travelled fast. Fiona wasn't stupid, she'd put two and two together and quickly realise that Darcy was waiting for Chloe.

Her only hope was to find Chloe and get her out of

sight, so they could have a conversation before anyone from management had a chance to kill her.

Darcy opened the door and stepped out into the communal area. As she did, Chloe stepped off the elevator. She was whistling a happy tune and swinging the satchel in her hand.

She has no idea, Darcy mused.

She walked forward and grabbed Chloe's arm. She turned them both around and marched towards the ladies' bathroom.

"Um, what's going on?" Chloe asked.

"You're about to be murdered," Darcy mumbled under her breath.

They both entered the bathroom, and Darcy quickly checked the cubicles to make sure they were alone.

"What do you mean?"

Darcy folded her arms and looked at Chloe. She looked baffled, big doe eyes at a loss.

"The podcast," Darcy explained. "You're in a lot of trouble. Helen is furious. Pippa wants your head on a spike. Fiona doesn't know yet, but she'll probably want to kill you as well. Or at least maim you."

"Why?" Chloe sagged against the sinks. "I was just trying to give *Honey* more exposure, let people know about it."

"You implied that *Honey* was in financial trouble," Darcy said.

Chloe's cheeks flushed. "Well, not really... I mean, I didn't really say anything."

"They said *Honey* was in trouble, whether or not *you* said it directly... that was the takeaway from the show."

"But *Honey is* in trouble," Chloe argued. "I know everyone is trying to keep it from the new girl, but I know we are."

"We are," Darcy agreed. "But it can't be made public knowledge. No business wants people to think they are in trouble. Even a whiff of financial problems creates big shockwaves. Advertisers will pull their ads, worried that the magazine won't make it to print. Shareholders and investors might try to pull their money out, meaning cashflow problems. It's a really big deal, Chloe."

Chloe's mouth hung open as she processed the situation.

"Not to mention that you gave a very public interview on behalf of *Honey* without telling anyone," Darcy added. "If you'd let Fiona know, she would have briefed you. Given you some kind of media training."

"I… I thought someone might try to go in my place," Chloe admitted. "And it was my friend, my contact, I wanted to take the credit." She stared at the ceiling and blew out a breath. "And now I'm going to lose my job because of it."

"You won't lose your job," Darcy said. "No point. The news is out there. Can't put the genie back in the bottle. You'll get a slap on the wrists and be told not to do it again."

Chloe pushed away from the sink. She wrapped her arms around her middle and started to pace.

"I listened to the show this morning, they cut so much stuff out. I talked about the digital edition and the great new deal we have running. I talked about the upcoming interviews and reviews. But they cut all of that out," Chloe said. "I just don't understand."

"I think your friend just wanted the inside scoop on *Honey*," Darcy said. "You say she was a friend?"

"Yeah, I knew her from university. We weren't exactly friends, but I knew her…"

"Did you ever upset her?" Darcy asked. "Because she really screwed you over. There's no way she wouldn't know that it would have a serious impact on *Honey*, and on you."

Chloe continued to pace. "I-I don't know. I don't think so. I… I hardly knew her."

Darcy wondered if there was something Chloe wasn't telling her. Or if Chloe genuinely didn't know. She seemed sincere, it was certainly possible that the host of the show had it in for her without her even realising. She resolved to do some research on Donna Hayward.

Chloe leaned against a wall. She tilted her head to the floor. "What do I do?"

Darcy shrugged. "Apologise. A lot. And ride it out. There's not a lot you can do. Hope that Helen and Fiona can convince people that we're not in trouble."

Chloe looked up slightly. "Pippa's going to be a nightmare, isn't she?"

"Yes," Darcy admitted. "Luckily, I know that she's due to leave the office for interviews around mid-morning. So, you only have to dodge her blows for a couple of hours."

"Thanks for warning me. I would have walked in there without a clue," Chloe admitted.

"It's okay. Just… be strong. And meet us for lunch in the kitchen and we'll cheer you up." Darcy had put her foot in it once or twice during her tenure at *Honey*. Not to the epic proportions Chloe had, but she knew a friendly face was essential to getting through those tough days.

"I owe you one," Chloe said.

"You do," Darcy agreed. "I'll let you know my payment terms when the occasion arises."

CHAPTER TWENTY-SIX

KIM WAS TYPING when she saw Chloe arrive. Chloe didn't so much walk into the office as quietly slink in, sliding into her chair as if hoping she had miraculously shrunk to an inch in height.

A split second after she had sat down, Kim's phone rang.

An internal call.

From Helen.

She picked up the handset.

"Get her in here," Helen said before Kim even had a chance to speak.

The line went dead. Kim put the handset down and stood up. She walked over to the digital department. Natasha hadn't arrived yet. Thankfully, Pippa was in the meeting room with Tess on a conference call. Fiona was on the phone, as she had been solidly since she got in. All good news that meant Chloe was still in one piece.

As she approached the desk, Chloe looked up at her sadly.

"Hey," Kim greeted.

"Hey," Chloe said miserably.

"Helen wants to see you."

"Yeah, Darcy said she would." Chloe stood up. "Shall we get it over with?"

Kim nodded. They both walked towards Helen's office. Chloe's cheeks were bright red and her eyes were wet with unshed tears. Kim wanted to hug her, tell her that it would be okay. But she knew that Chloe was barely holding it together.

They approached Helen's open office door. Chloe hesitated. Kim stepped around her and into the office.

"Chloe's here," she announced.

Helen continued to focus on her monitor. She lifted her hand and pointed to a chair opposite her desk. Chloe hurried into the room and sat down.

"Kim, did you hear the podcast last night?" Helen asked without looking up.

"Yes."

"Then you should be here, too. Close the door behind you."

Damn, twice in one week, Kim thought. She stepped into the office and closed the door. She took the seat beside Chloe. Helen continued typing, finishing up whatever she was doing.

The office was quiet except for the loud clacking of the keyboard, each letter pierced the silence like a gunshot. Chloe's knee started bouncing.

Finally, Helen reached for the mouse and clicked a button. She removed her glasses and turned to face Chloe.

"I didn't hear the podcast," Helen started. "I'm not one

of the tens of thousands of people who apparently listen to it. While I'm aware that I should *now* listen to it, I sadly don't have time to. Because I'm receiving around five emails a minute from investors, shareholders, sister publications, advertisers, journalists, and more.

"From what I understand, you were interviewed on a podcast last night? One with a very large audience. And it was said that *Honey* is in financial difficulty, is that true?"

"The host pushed her," Kim jumped in. "Chloe didn't actually say anything like that. Not directly."

"I said that all magazines were experiencing a dip in sales," Chloe confessed. "And I said that *Honey* had experienced a decline in readership. I'm so sorry."

"Do you understand why we wouldn't want that information to be public knowledge?" Helen asked.

"I didn't. But I do now. I was just trying to help; my friend runs the podcast. I thought if I could speak to her about *Honey*, the word would get out there and more people would be aware of it and hopefully buy it." Chloe ran her palms over her skirt.

Helen leaned back in her chair. "It was a very irresponsible thing to do. You do *not* speak for *Honey*. And it goes without saying that private financial information is not to be shared outside this office."

"O-of course. I would never give information like that. I was… I just wanted people to know about *Honey*. The show was edited to make it sound a lot worse than it was." Chloe stopped and sucked in a deep breath. "As I say, I'm very sorry. I… I understand if I'm fired."

Kim wanted to melt into the floor on Chloe's behalf.

"You're not fired," Helen said. "You made a mistake. If

we all got fired for making mistakes there wouldn't be a solvent company in the world. But there will be a lot of work now; damage control."

Chloe nodded. "If I can help in anyway—"

"You can promise me to never do a podcast ever again." Helen's stare was hard and cold. She may have decided to give Chloe a second chance, but it was still clear that she was furious with her.

"Oh, trust me, I've learnt my lesson. I don't think I'll even *listen* to a podcast *ever* again."

Helen stared at her for a few long moments. The tension in the air was thick. Kim had never seen Helen so angry in the office. Irritated, sure. Peeved, definitely. Angry? Never. It wasn't something she wanted to see again.

"Go back to your desk. Don't contact your friend anymore. Don't speak to anyone without my permission," Helen instructed.

Chloe jumped to her feet and rushed out of the office, closing the door behind her.

"Her heart was in the right place," Kim defended.

"Clearly her thought process wasn't." Helen leaned forward and interlaced her fingers. "You heard it; how was it?"

Kim winced. "Not good. She wasn't on for long and the host, Donna, kept pushing that *Honey* was in trouble. Chloe didn't exactly confirm or deny anything, but by then the damage was already done."

"She said it was edited?" Helen asked.

"Yes, the show was recorded last night and then edited and uploaded. Obviously, I don't know what was edited out, but I felt it sounded like the host was fishing for dirt. I don't think Chloe is stupid, I believe her if she says it sounded a lot worse than what she said."

Helen nodded. "Very well. Do you know if Lucy heard it?"

Kim nodded. "She immediately started drafting replies to the messages she knew she'd get today. I think a couple of her new clients are considering pulling their advertising, but I know she'll get them back."

Kim hoped she sounded confident. She didn't feel it. Lucy had been in a blind panic the night before, convinced that her job was really hanging by a thread now.

"I hope so." Helen stretched her arms in the air. Her back popped. She slumped back into her chair. "I have a meeting with Celia this afternoon, apparently she listens to the show, which I don't mind telling you surprises me a great deal."

"Is she angry?" Kim made a mental note to tell Darcy about Celia's expected visit.

"Celia doesn't really get angry. She's… concerned. She's an investor, and while she's not stupid enough to panic and pull her funds, she could be caught in the crossfire if other investors do."

Helen's attention was caught by something on her screen. She sighed. "I'll be happy to get away from my emails for an hour. You'd think the world was ending."

"Can I do anything?" Kim asked hopefully. She wanted to help. She felt like she was partially to blame. She knew that Chloe was doing the show and had kept it a secret for her. Not that she'd willingly admit that to anyone. No, she'd keep her guilt to herself. It had company, and her secrets were forming a stomach ulcer to swim in.

"No, we're a little beyond canned responses. Just keep taking messages for any phone calls that come in. And block out my diary from two onward for this meeting with Celia. Oh, is Fiona in?"

"Yes, she's been on the phone since she got in. I think she's having the same issues you are."

"Any news on whether or not we have a photographer?"

Kim shook her head. "I've not heard anything or seen Nicola."

"Okay. This little disaster buys Fiona a little more time." Helen sat forward and pulled the laptop towards her. "Thanks, Kim. That's all for now."

Kim stood up. "What happens if she can't convince Nicola to come back?"

"My ex will get the house, because I'll be in prison for murder," Helen deadpanned.

CHAPTER TWENTY-SEVEN

CHLOE NEVER THOUGHT she would be so grateful for Natasha's silent nature. But here she was, a few days into her new job, hanging by a thread and relishing her boss' absolute silence.

When Natasha arrived, she'd simply raised her eyebrow at Chloe and shook her head with disappointment. Then she'd taken her seat and emailed Chloe her tasks for the day, much the same as any other day. It was a relief. She'd gladly take the cold shoulder over the disappointment she'd seen in Helen's eyes.

However, a raised eyebrow and a shake of the head wasn't Pippa's approach. An expletive-filled rant had been her choice, until Wendy had ushered Chloe away under the guise of helping her with some paperwork.

Thankfully, Pippa had soon left the office for her interviews. It took some of the heat off, but she was still well aware of the glares from Fiona and Lucy that pierced the back of her head like hot pokers. At least they hated her silently.

She half-wished that Helen had fired her. She'd be on the way to her parents' house to be bathed in tea and sympathy. She'd be jobless and having to beg the accountancy firm for the job offer that had probably gone to someone more qualified by now. But at least she wouldn't be the most hated person in *Honey*.

The difference a few hours made. She'd started the day thinking she'd be the company's saviour, now she was sure she had sealed its fate. She'd considered walking back into Helen's office and offering her resignation. But then she wondered if that was a little like offering to pay the ransom after the hostages had died of old age.

She sensed movement beside her and jumped.

Tess looked down at her and grinned. "Don't worry, I've not been sent to take you out." She pulled up a chair and sat close to Chloe. She leaned in and whispered, "How are you doing?"

"Awful," Chloe admitted. "Everyone hates me, and I've done something really stupid that might damage the company."

Tess waved her hand as if it wasn't the worst day of Chloe's life to date. "Everyone doesn't hate you. They're annoyed at you, but it will pass."

"That doesn't make me feel any better," Chloe pointed out.

"On my first day at *Honey*, I set fire to the office," Tess said casually. She leaned forward and plucked a stapler from the desk and started to play with it.

Click, click, click.

Chloe blinked. "A… fire?"

"Yep. Flames. Fire engines. The works. In fact, I think the word *blaze* was used. I left my cardigan, my favourite cardigan I might add, on a heater in the meeting room. This is the old office, not here. Anyway. It caught fire… sprinklers started shooting water everywhere. Disaster."

Click, click, click. Tess played with the stapler, staring at the ceiling, deep in recollection.

Chloe's heart pounded at the very thought of not only a fire but being the one who started it.

"The head fire officer came out with the burnt, soaked remnants of my cardigan," Tess continued. She lowered her gaze and looked at Chloe seriously. "Every single member of staff turned to look at me."

Chloe gasped. The visual was enough to make her feel sick with nerves. "What did you do?"

Tess put the stapler back on the desk. "Kept my head down and did my job. We moved into a temporary office, the insurance paid for everything we lost. Except the work. God, the extra hours everyone had to put in to get that issue out. But we got there. And over time… people forgot about it."

"Really?" Chloe didn't imagine many people would forget that.

"Well, they do except for when I tell the story to make people feel better about their own mistakes." Tess chuckled. "I know it doesn't seem like it right now, but things will sort themselves out."

Chloe shook her head. "I don't think so. Helen is pretty angry with me. Can you really have a successful career in a company when your boss' boss thinks you're an idiot?"

Tess shrugged her shoulders. "I don't know. But let's find out together."

Chloe felt her lips curling in a smile. The first in a number of hours.

"Do your job. Do it to the best of your ability. That was why you were hired; you're good at your job and we need your skillset. So, do your job. Everything else will take care of itself."

Chloe slowly inclined her head. "Thanks, Tess. I appreciate that."

"No problem." Tess stood up and put her hand on Chloe's shoulder. "Oh, and don't remind Helen about the whole fire thing. I genuinely think she's forgotten."

CHAPTER TWENTY-EIGHT

Darcy opened Helen's shared online calendar. She grimaced. Helen had changed her privacy preferences, or Kim had. People could see when she was in a meeting, but not any details about what the meeting was. Or, most relevant to Darcy, *where* the meeting was.

Kim had kindly braved the icy cold of the marketing department to whisper to her that a lunch meeting was happening, so she knew Helen was meeting Celia somewhere at two. But she didn't know if Celia was coming into the office or if Helen was meeting her somewhere else.

The thick air of tension had made for a silent morning. Rose had kept her head down and got on with her work, and Kim had only briefly spoken to her all day. She was relieved. It meant no one had time to quiz her about the evening before. She didn't need their pitying looks when she told them that everything had gone wrong.

Her confidence had taken a big knock. She no longer wanted to bump into Celia and speak with her. No, she'd settle for her usual tactic of watching the impressive woman from afar. It would take a few weeks for her to build her confidence back up to even consider a new plan for approaching Celia directly. Or rather, putting herself in Celia's path and hoping that she was approached.

For now, she was back to doing whatever she could to get a distant glimpse of Celia. Even if she was painfully aware that her actions were decidedly stalker-like. She shook the thought from her head.

"Fiona?" Darcy spoke up once her boss came off the telephone.

Fiona looked up. Her eyes were glazed over, and she looked exhausted. Darcy couldn't blame her, she'd be on the phone non-stop, repeating the same things and trying to sound jovial and relaxed while she did.

"Can I go for lunch at two today?" Darcy asked.

Fiona nodded. Her phone rang, and she sighed. "That's fine," she said before answering the call.

Rose turned to face her. "Lunch plans?" she pouted.

"Not exactly, just going for a walk."

Rose paused for a moment before understanding dawned. "Oh… I see. Helen was talking about wanting to try the new French bistro place that opened up near Berkeley Square."

Darcy grinned. "Thanks, that sounds like a good area to check out."

Lucy slammed her phone down and stalked away from her desk. She thundered past the digital desks, glaring at Chloe as she did.

Darcy raised her eyebrows at the display.

"Advertisers are dropping like flies," Rose explained. "All

the new accounts she'd nearly secured have said they're leaving, or they want a substantial discount."

Darcy toyed with the elastic band ball on her desk.

"Sinking ship," Rose whispered.

"Not yet," Darcy murmured back.

Rose returned to her work. Darcy knew it didn't look good, but she hoped it would just be temporary. *Honey's* potential failure was today's news, but hopefully something else would come along tomorrow.

Fiona had been on the phone all morning talking figures and laughing at claims they were about to file for bankruptcy. She sounded convincing. She'd convinced Darcy, even though Darcy knew there was financial trouble. But that was why Fiona was so good at her job.

Lucy had been busy sweet-talking advertisers but with a hint of stress in her tone. Darcy couldn't blame her. Lucy's entire job revolved around getting ad revenue into the business. Watching them all leave suddenly for no reason would cause anyone to have palpitations.

She squeezed the elastic band ball fiercely. She didn't want *Honey* to go under. She loved this crazy little group of people. Well, not Pippa maybe, but everyone else. And of course, she couldn't stand the thought of not seeing Celia again.

Chloe stood up to go to the bathroom. She cast a quick glance over towards the marketing desks. Darcy offered her a smile. The poor lass looked like she was close to tears. She couldn't imagine how today must feel for her.

It will all pass over, she reminded herself. *It has to.*

CHAPTER TWENTY-NINE

FIONA LOWERED the handset and stabbed the button to send her calls to voicemail. She needed a break, just five minutes. Endless calls from journalists, suppliers, and investors had given her a sore throat.

She clicked the refresh button on her emails. A wave of new messages arrived, but nothing from Nicola. She regretted sending her note that morning. She should have said more, apologised more, offered a solution. Calling herself an idiot, while accurate, wasn't enough.

But she didn't have time to dwell on yet another failure on the Nicola front. The PR storm that Chloe had created wasn't going away anytime soon. She opened an email from Rose, one of many that had been sent to her throughout the morning. It detailed yet another thread on *Honey*'s imminent failure. She rolled her eyes and marked it as unread. Something to deal with later.

She heard a noise, a low rumbling. She turned around in her chair and saw Wendy, with a mug of tea in each hand, wheeling the office chair she sat in ever closer to her. She looked ridiculous.

"Now, I know you must be parched after all that gassing," Wendy said.

Fiona wasn't quite happy with the phrase *gassing*, but she was thirsty.

Wendy parked her chair beside Fiona's and handed her a mug.

"Thank you," Fiona said. She took a sip of the beverage. She had to admit, Wendy made the best tea.

"Are you okay?" Wendy asked, slurping her own tea.

"Yes, slowly getting to speak to everyone," Fiona replied. She knew that it was primarily down to her and Helen to calm the flames. People were relying on her, and it wouldn't do to be showing her concerns.

"I don't mean about this business." Wendy waved her hand dismissively as if the potential ruin of the company was nothing. "I mean *you*."

"Me?" Fiona asked. She stared at Wendy, wondering why on earth she was asking. "I'm fine, really."

"Hmm." Wendy didn't sound like she believed her. "What about this Nicola business?"

Fiona laughed, half-heartedly. "She was overreacting to a… a misunderstanding. And now I have to soothe her fragile ego. It'll be fine."

She sipped some more tea, trying to distract from the fact that she had no idea if it would be fine or not. She hoped it would be. A financial pinch in the form of the sudden need to buy expensive stock photography and get a new photographer wasn't going to help *Honey*'s current predicament.

"It must be hard on you," Wendy said. "Saying something that hurt someone's feelings, even though you didn't mean it. I know you like Nicola. We all do. My brother is like you, always saying the wrong thing to people he cares most about. It's like his brain splutters and then he says something he didn't mean to."

Fiona put the mug down, afraid that her shaking hand might spill tea down her blouse. Wendy had struck right on the issue. And it scared her. Was she that transparent?

"But everyone who knows him knows his heart is in the right place. They don't take offence. Maybe you need to give Nicola a chance to get to know you? Then she'd just brush it off when you say something you don't mean."

"I don't think I have much say in that," Fiona admitted. "I've insulted her enough times that I'm sure she doesn't want to get to know me."

"That's not true," Wendy assured her.

"I think it is. I… I tried to apologise, and she's not replied. I'm not surprised, I don't think I'd accept my apology either."

"Give her time." Wendy patted her hand.

Fiona didn't like someone feeling sorry for her, even if Wendy was well meaning. The stress of the morning coupled with the Nicola business, and now Wendy's caring concern, made her feel like she was on the edge of tears.

She pushed her chair back from her desk.

"I'm sorry, I have to head out. I'll be back later." She grabbed her handbag and hurried across the office. She didn't know where she was going, just that she needed some fresh air and some time alone. She pulled the door to the communal area open and nearly walked right into Nicola.

She stopped, frozen in place.

Nicola stood in front of her in ripped jeans and a tank top, camera bag slung casually over her shoulder. She was… smiling. She seemed happy to see her.

Fiona swallowed nervously.

"Hey, I was just coming to see you."

Fiona frowned. She hadn't expected Nicola in the office. Certainly not to see her. And definitely not with a smile.

"Um."

"Do you have time for a coffee?" Nicola asked.

"I don't drink coffee." She winced. She wanted to slap herself. Why couldn't she have a normal conversation with this woman?

"Okay…" Nicola chuckled. "Do you have time for a refreshing beverage of your choice? I presume you drink liquid?"

Fiona grinned. "I do, yes."

Nicola tilted her head and smiled playfully. "So? Do you have some time?"

She looked into the office. Wendy stood to the side, out of sight of Nicola but close enough to be able to hear everything. She gave Fiona a cheesy thumbs-up.

Fiona laughed and shook her head.

"I do."

CHAPTER THIRTY

A BLUR RUSHED out of Helen's office and parked itself in front of Kim's desk.

"If anyone calls for me, take a message. Unless it's Christine, in which case tell her I'll call her back and then text me immediately." Helen dropped her mobile phone into her handbag and closed the flap.

Kim nodded. She plucked a tissue from her desk and held it out. With her other hand she tapped the left-hand corner of her mouth.

Helen took the tissue and removed the smudge of lipstick. She screwed up the tissue and threw it in the bin beneath Kim's desk.

"Going anywhere nice?" Kim fished, hoping to get some intel for Darcy.

"No idea, she's meeting me outside." Helen looked at her watch. "Call me if anything urgent comes up."

"Will do." Kim waited for Helen to leave before jumping to her feet. Darcy would have to hurry if she was going to tail the two women wherever they were going. She walked around her desk and nearly straight into Pippa.

"Hi," Kim said, taking a step back. "Interviews done?"

Pippa narrowed her eyes.

Something was up.

"I received the most interesting phone call," Pippa started. She folded her arms. "A friend who works at a rival magazine had a call from Lucy about a position they have."

"So?" Kim was already out off kilter at seeing Pippa glare at her. Now she knew why she worried her heard might beat out of her chest.

"Your girlfriend is looking for alternative employment," Pippa elaborated.

"It's a free country," Kim defended. "If she wants to look at other jobs, that's her business."

Pippa smirked. Like a tiger with its prey in sight.

"When my friend asked why she was looking for a new job, why she was considering leaving *Honey*, Lucy said that she had information that caused her to think that she would be asked to leave soon." Pippa planted her hands on her hips. "Considering this all happened before that brainless blonde in digital told the UK's largest lesbian podcast that we're effectively destitute, I'd be interested to know how Lucy came to that conclusion."

Kim's palms started to sweat. She folded her arms and glared back at Pippa.

"Are you suggesting something?"

"Why, yes, I am. I'm suggesting that *confidential* information might have been made available to your *girlfriend*." Pippa raised an eyebrow, daring Kim to argue.

Kim did her best shocked impression, hoping it would

stand up to Pippa's intense scrutiny. "Are you insinuating something?"

"You know exactly what I'm insinuating. Maybe we should discuss this with Helen?" Pippa pressed.

"She's out to lunch. And there's nothing to discuss."

Kim had started to panic. Pippa was like a dog with a bone at the best of times. There was no way she'd let this go. Helen may be at lunch now, but she'd be back soon. And she'd see straight through Kim's lies.

Should Kim admit to it? Would that make it better? Could anything make it better?

"Excuse me." Tess stepped into the conversation. "Couldn't help but overhear, since, you know, you're shouting. I thought I better say that it was me."

Pippa spun to look at her colleague. "What was you?"

"I told Lucy that she might be made redundant," Tess said.

Kim felt her mouth drop open in shock, but quickly slammed it shut again.

"What? You…" Pippa was as flummoxed as Kim.

"I overheard it and I warned Lucy. I know she's been struggling with money and her family have disowned her. I didn't want her to suddenly be made redundant and have no backup plan."

Tess folded her arms and sat on the corner of Kim's desk. "I remember when I was her age, my parents were supportive. Well, they didn't throw me out. They didn't do cartwheels either. But I had them, and I still have them. I can't imagine being her age and having no one. Can you?" She looked pointedly at Pippa.

Pippa looked from Kim to Tess and back again.

"Her personal situation is of no matter to me. The distribution of confidential information in this office is completely out of control," Pippa raged.

"It is," Tess agreed. "I'll tell Helen what I did the moment she comes back."

"Well, there's no need to do anything rash," Pippa said. "Just be more careful with confidential information in the future. I won't say anything, this time," she warned. "But be careful. Loose lips sink ships."

"If you think that's best, Pip. Absolutely. I'll keep quiet if I hear anything else in the future," Tess promised.

Pippa let out a sigh that sounded almost like a growl and hurried away.

Kim sagged against her desk. "Thanks," she whispered to Tess.

"It's okay, she'd happily throw you under a bus, but she needs me," Tess said. "Just be careful in the future."

Kim hated that Pippa had such a high opinion of herself but such disgusting double standards. Tess was absolutely right, she'd think nothing of having most of the staff fired. But Pippa needed Tess, she was one of the few people who could work with Pippa without crying, quitting, or threatening to sue.

"I will. Trust me, I feel terrible about warning her and gossiping," Kim confessed. She still felt sick to her stomach whenever she thought about how much Helen placed her trust in her, and how she had broken that trust when she had the chance.

"I would have done the same if I'd been in your position. You can't keep that kind of information from your girlfriend," Tess said. "Just, you know, don't do it again."

Kim nodded quickly. "I won't. It's eating me alive!"

Tess regarding her seriously. "Well, don't tell Helen, either. She has too much on her plate right now, and she needs you, Kim. I think you're the only reason she has remained in one piece these last few months. She relies on you."

"I know." Kim sat back down. "That's what makes it so much harder. One minute, I think I can't live with the guilt anymore. But then I know that it will be worse for Helen if I tell her. I'd absolve my guilt but leave her with no one to trust."

She leaned forward and put her head in her hands. "I didn't mean to do it. It was an accident. Well, I mean… I did it. Obviously. No one held a gun to my head. But it was a split-second decision. I didn't go looking for it."

Tess placed her hand on Kim's shoulder. "I know, honey. No one would think of you as malicious. We've all been in a situation where we know we'll upset someone, but we have to do it, or we'll upset someone else."

Kim tilted her head and looked up at Tess. "I feel like a really bad person. And my heart nearly stopped when Pippa said that. What if Helen does find out?"

"Then she finds out."

Kim shuddered. "That doesn't make me feel any better."

"Deal with what happens when it happens," Tess told her. She patted Kim on the shoulder again before standing up. "No point in worrying about things you can't change."

CHAPTER THIRTY-ONE

FIONA DIDN'T WANT the tea that sat in front of her. But she didn't like coffee, and ordering hot chocolate just seemed childish. So, she ordered tea. That she didn't want.

The reason she'd panic-ordered tea sat opposite her, hands wrapped around a mug containing an overly complicated coffee order.

They'd silently walked out of the building and to the nearest coffee shop. They'd queued without saying a word. The first time either spoke was to offer to pay for the other's drink. Fiona had won that short argument. She'd stared at the boy behind the till and told *him* that she'd be paying. He'd quickly taken Fiona's card payment.

They'd found a small table in the corner and sat down. They couldn't be silent any longer. Whatever they were going to say was soon to come out.

Fiona didn't know why Nicola had come to the office, why she wanted to talk. She curled her hands up in her lap and stared at the wall, awaiting the series of misunderstandings they were no doubt about to have. She'd already resigned herself to Nicola leaving *Honey*. Helen's insistence that she fix it was foolish. Fiona couldn't fix it. Surely, Helen had noticed that Fiona just couldn't communicate with Nicola? Helen was more astute than she let on.

"So," Nicola said, "you apologise for being... now, what was it?" She grinned, looking up to the ceiling as if trying to recall the exact wording.

Fiona rolled her eyes. "A rude and inconsiderate arse."

"That was it." Nicola took a sip of her drink.

"You have an electronic copy of it, did you really need to drag me down here to get me to repeat it?" Fiona asked. She was annoyed that Nicola seemed to be mocking her. Okay, her email wasn't the best thought-out in the world. But it was from the heart.

"Sorry, I didn't mean to be flippant," Nicola said sincerely. "I dragged you down here to say that you're not an idiot. Or rude. Or inconsiderate. Or an arse."

Fiona wasn't sure she had heard correctly. She gripped her hands even tighter in her lap.

"I feel like it," she confessed. "I don't know why I reacted the way I did. I could make up some excuse about the heat, but I really just don't know what came over me."

Nicola inclined her head in agreement. "It did seem very unlike you."

"It was." She reached forward and took a sip of tea. She grimaced, it really wasn't what she wanted. "So... Helen told me that you've left *Honey*?"

Nicola shrugged. "I did, but now I'm not sure. I was angry and... well. What else did Helen say?"

"Helen ordered me to get you back," Fiona admitted.

Nicola chuckled. "Sounds like her. And how do you plan to do that?" She leaned back and folded her arms, looking at Fiona with interest. Her eyes twinkled with mischief.

"Well, I've given it some thought. I don't think you'd be open to outright bribery." She reached for a cardboard sales message on the table and toyed with it. "If I talk about how talented you are, I don't think you'd believe me, following... you know."

"After you said that my work was shocking? Or was it abysmal?" Nicola supplied.

"I believe I said both, actually."

"Oh, yes, that's right." Nicola took another sip of her drink.

Fiona noted that she was still smiling. She didn't quite know what that meant, but she was grateful for it. Hopefully, Nicola was just going to tease her for a bit and then agree to come back. Could she be that lucky?

"So, I'm not sure I have anything to offer you, other than my apologies," Fiona continued.

"For being a rude, inconsiderate arse?" Nicola asked.

Fiona's lips curled into a smile. "Yes, for *that*. Will we be repeating it much more?"

"Probably, it's got a nice ring to it," Nicola said. "I might be convinced to come back, if you agree to something."

Fiona dropped the marketing messaging and discreetly dried her sweaty palms on her skirt. She felt like she was on a knife's edge, waiting to say the wrong thing. It had been the longest period of time she had spoken to Nicola without a terrible miscalculation. Surely it had to go wrong soon.

Especially with Nicola being in a playful mood, clearly enjoying Fiona's nerves.

"That depends on what it is," Fiona said. She couldn't imagine what Nicola might possibly want from her. Maybe something terribly demeaning?

"Nothing too terrible. On Friday nights, I volunteer at a children's activity centre. I help kids learn about art and photography. If you come with me this Friday night, I'll come back to *Honey*." Nicola leaned back on her chair and pinned Fiona with a cocky smile.

Fiona's eyes widened in horror. "Me? What can I possibly do to help? I'm, I'm useless with children. How old are these children? A-and I don't know anything. I'm… Why?"

Nicola held her hands up. "Whoa, whoa. It's okay. Chill, chill. You're not going to be in charge of the kids, there's plenty of adult supervision. I just want you to come along, it's something that's important to me. And, what with you being a rude and inconsiderate arse—"

"You're not going to let that go, are you?"

"—I think it might be something you'd get some benefit out of. Volunteering. Helping the community. Learning about art. What do you say? You can carry my bag."

Fiona couldn't help but smile. "Carry your bag? How generous."

"I know. There's over three thousand pounds' worth of equipment in my bag."

Suddenly, Fiona didn't feel qualified to even carry the bag.

Nicola leaned forward. "We'll be there for two hours

tops. Children have to be in bed early, did you know? No partying until midnight."

"No, really?" Fiona played along. "So, they won't be clubbing with us later?"

"Maybe Annie, she's a troublemaker," Nicola said. "I'd like to see you clubbing, by the way."

Fiona felt her cheeks heat. She coughed and lowered her head, keen to avoid Nicola's gaze.

"I don't go clubbing, as I'm sure you know."

"Shame. Anyway, will you do it? Will you broaden your horizons and give me a hand, all in one go?"

"Why?"

Nicola laughed. "Wow, you don't hold back, do you?"

Fiona winced. She probably could have phrased it better. She sipped at her tea again. It was going cold and bitter. She fished the teabag out and placed it on the saucer. It was too late now; the liquid was almost black.

"I was terrible to you, why do you want to spend more time with me?" Fiona clarified. "Unless these children are little demons and it's a form of punishment?"

Nicola's grin was so wide that anyone watching them would have been under the misconception that they were having immense fun. Fiona wondered if Nicola was. She certainly seemed to be enjoying herself. Did she like making Fiona squirm?

"It's not punishment," Nicola tried to reassure her, though the grin wasn't helping. "I just want to get to know you outside of *Honey*. Nothing nefarious. I just… I know most people at *Honey* pretty well. Even Pippa. But you're a bit of a mystery. I like to know who I'm working with. And I honestly think you'll enjoy it. There's nothing scary about it. You can sit in the corner of the room if you like. I won't make you interact with anyone. Just… come along."

Fiona really couldn't fathom why Nicola wanted her to go. Whatever the reason was, it wouldn't become clear until she went.

Which she knew she had to do.

"I don't really have much choice, do I?" Fiona asked.

"Not really," Nicola admitted.

CHAPTER THIRTY-TWO

IT WAS VERY NEARLY the end of Darcy's lunch hour, and she hadn't caught sight of Helen and Celia. Nor had she eaten anything.

She'd missed the two women leaving the office when she was stuck on a call. In her distraction, she'd not noticed that it had been a call for Fiona which had bounced to her. It took ten minutes to get the journalist off the phone. He kept asking questions and requesting a quote from her. By the time she had finally gotten rid of him, she'd all but run from the office. She'd looked up and down the bustling street, but there had been no sign of them.

Taking Rose's advice, she headed first for Berkeley Square. The hot day meant that everyone was dining outside, which made her task a lot easier. She'd quickly checked out the main spots in Berkeley Square and surrounding areas before heading down to Green Park. She knew that Helen liked to dine at the May Fair and the Ritz. Luckily, the grand hotels were used to strangers traversing their halls, and no one looked twice as Darcy entered the lobbies, looked into the restaurants, and then left again.

As time ticked by, she became more manic. She felt like a mother searching for her lost child. She knew it wasn't healthy, but she couldn't stop herself. She didn't know what it was about Celia that made a madwoman out of her.

Darcy prided herself on always being pragmatic, balanced, and sensible. But when Celia came into the picture, she operated on some deranged autopilot that saw her acting in a way she didn't recognise.

She looked at her watch; it had been fifty minutes and she hadn't seen either woman anywhere. It was time to get back to the office, and time to grab a bite to eat. She was near the Langham and knew she'd have to hurry to get back to the office in time. Something that didn't appeal in the continued heat.

Regent Street was crammed with people, even as far north as she was. If she tried to fight her way through the crowd she would definitely be late. Darcy wasn't usually picky about things like that, but she didn't want to push her luck on an already tense day.

She ducked down a side street and picked up the pace. The Langham had been a last-ditch effort that she now wished she hadn't bothered with. It was outside of her usual roaming area, and she hadn't quite realised how long it would take to get there.

She rushed past upmarket restaurants, offices, delivery hubs, banks, and gyms. She mentally kicked herself for not having bought lunch at the start of her journey. Now she couldn't find anywhere to pick up a grab-and-go meal.

Never do this again, she told herself. But she knew the

chance of getting a glimpse of Celia in the future would no doubt have her repeating today's mistake.

She was a few streets away from the office when she found a sandwich shop. It wasn't the type of place she'd often go in, but she knew the branded stores by the office would have long queues of tourists.

Going to the gallery the previous evening meant she had eaten out. If she'd stayed home, she would have cooked a nice meal and portioned some of it to take to work the next day. As if she needed another reason to beat herself up about the whole gallery debacle.

Why did you pick today to not bring a homemade lunch? she asked herself as she looked at the most lacklustre display of limp sandwiches she had ever seen. Her stomach grumbled at the prospect of eating a curly cheese sandwich.

She picked up a chicken tikka sandwich, it looked the most appealing. She grabbed a bottle of water and cursed herself for not bringing her water bottle and hydration tracker with her. The day really was going to hell.

"Sorry, I've run out of bags," the shop assistant told her. He didn't seem sorry at all.

"That's fine." She paid for the sandwich and water and hurried out of the shop.

She'd have to eat at her desk. It wasn't ideal but luckily people at *Honey* weren't that strict about things. Rose would no doubt make a comment about the smell, but Darcy would remind her about her Friday curry habit in the winter months.

The traffic lights were red, and so she ran across the main road, seeing the *Honey* building in the distance. She'd be a couple of minutes late but that was all. She held the sandwich under her arm and screwed the cap off the water bottle. It was too hot to carry on rushing around without a drink. She took a few hefty swigs of water and then let out a sigh.

She put the cap back on and looked up to see Helen and Celia standing right outside the office. Her eyes widened. There was no way around them. They were in front of the revolving door, deep in conversation about something.

She couldn't imagine what she must look like. Exhausted, sweaty, manic. Now was the worst possible time to bump into Celia. She wondered if she could hide for a few moments?

Before she had a chance to decide what to do, Helen noticed her. She smiled and nodded her head in greeting. "Hello, Darcy. Late lunch?"

"H-hi," she stammered. She looked down at her half-crushed sandwich. "Yeah."

"Yeah?" Is that all I have? Why do I have to bump into Celia now, when I have a disgusting, shop-bought sandwich on white bread? Why not last night when I was prepared and looked flawless?

Celia was looking at her with a polite smile. She was actually looking at her. For the first time Celia Fox's full attention was on Darcy. And Darcy had no idea what to do.

"Did you listen to the podcast?" Helen enquired.

Darcy nodded.

Helen rolled her eyes. "Seems that everyone but me has heard it. What did you make of it?"

Darcy blinked. She couldn't believe her bad luck. She had spent the last hour looking for these very two women, just so she could see them from afar. She certainly didn't want to talk to them. Definitely not now, when she no doubt looked a mess from running around in the heat for the past hour. And now, Helen wanted to *talk* to her. To ask her opinion on something very important. Something that she ordinarily would be able to do with no problem at all, but something that seemed so impossible now that Celia's eyes were upon her.

"The host... seemed to have an agenda," Darcy said. "Chloe said that a lot of what she said was edited out."

"Who is the host?" Helen asked.

"Someone called Donna Hayward," Celia supplied.

"She went to university with Chloe, but I don't think they were that close," Darcy said.

Helen nodded. "I see. Well, I'll let you get on with your lunch, thank you."

Darcy quickly turned and all but threw herself into the revolving door to escape the situation. She unleashed an internal scream to stop herself from thinking too much about what just happened and how stupid she probably looked.

Her hurried steps started to slow. She paused and turned around. Helen and Celia were still talking outside.

Going back out there wasn't at all appealing, but she had to say her piece, just in case it made a difference. She took a deep breath and walked back outside again.

"Helen? I'm sorry for interrupting," she said.

Helen looked at her quizzically.

Darcy focused her attention on Helen. If she looked at Celia now she would melt into the pavement.

"I... I think this can be fixed," Darcy said.

Helen grinned. "I'm open to any suggestions."

"The LBT community, our main core of readers, are very supportive. We're used to fighting for what we believe in. We're great at organising and rallying to a cause. I think we need to tell the community the truth."

Helen opened her mouth, probably to disagree.

"Hear me out," Darcy requested. "We tell people that we're not in trouble but that things aren't great. We play on *Honey*'s history, and its unique position in our culture. We say that *Honey* is here today, but it might not be here tomorrow. Or, rather *Honey* is here now, but it might not be in five years. We remind people how they felt when they first realised they weren't alone, how they felt a part of something when they picked up a copy of *Honey* and recognised themselves in its pages."

Helen and Celia shared a look. They didn't seem horrified by the idea.

Darcy took a deep breath and continued. "It's like with social media; technology turns businesses into brands. People are more likely to connect with a brand, or an ideal, than they are a business. We need to push that brand, remind people of *Honey*. The podcast could be the start of a new campaign, remembering *Honey* from when you were young. Start a conversation about the future, and how *Honey* might not be there for LBTs in the future."

Out of the corner of her eye, she saw Celia nod her head. She was clearly interested in the idea. Darcy's heart soared. There had been a very real chance that they would think she was being foolish or idealistic. And that would have been the end of any chance of impressing Celia in the future. She'd forever be the stupid girl with the naïve plan. But she seemed to be convincing them.

"We could tell the advertisers that it is part of a campaign. Hell, we could make it part of a campaign," Darcy said, now that she'd gained momentum. "We're not really in trouble, we know that our community fights for what it believes in, we're using that knowledge to stoke a fire."

Helen held up her hand to calm Darcy down. "I get what you're saying. I'll need to think about it in a little more detail, but I like what I'm hearing. I think you may be onto something."

Darcy smiled widely. She took her focus from Helen for a moment and looked at Celia. Celia was grinning at her. She looked impressed.

Darcy's breath caught. She tried to suck up the feeling of being the centre of Celia's attention. She wanted to remember forever the day that Celia looked at her and saw her for more than just a girl in the office. The day Celia realised that she had a voice, she had ideas.

"What do you think?" Helen asked Celia.

"I like it," Celia said. "As you say, we need to consider it from all angles. But I think it's worth exploring. Thank you... Darcy, was it?"

Darcy felt like she could die happy. Celia Fox knew her name. And had heard her say something reasonably intelligent.

Darcy nodded.

"Darcy Quinn works with Fiona," Helen explained. "She's a very astute marketer, an essential part of the team. Oh, and she makes granola bars that are to die for."

Darcy was relieved for her already red cheeks from the rush back to the office. Surely that meant she couldn't blush anymore now?

Celia raised an eyebrow. "Sounds divine, save one for me next time."

"Thank you, Darcy," Helen said. "Don't let us keep you from your lunch."

Both women looked at the soggy, cling-film-wrapped mess that Darcy had gripped in her hand.

"Oh, this is for Rose," she lied. "I've had my salmon and brown rice salad ages ago. But I better get this to her before she keels over."

She turned around and walked through the revolving doors with as much sway in her hips as she could manage.

Nailed it.

CHAPTER THIRTY-THREE

CHLOE WAS ANXIOUSLY LOOKING FORWARD to the day being over. She'd already decided that she was going to blow her weekly food budget on a greasy pizza, eat it all, and then go to bed. The sooner the day was done, the better.

She'd managed to avoid talking to anyone but Natasha for most of the afternoon. Pippa had gone out again, for which everyone was grateful. Helen had her office door closed, which seemed to be unusual, and everyone else was busily, quietly getting on with work.

It was a weird environment, one that Chloe wasn't used to. She'd often worked in large, open-plan offices with a staff in excess of a hundred people. There was never a suffocating air in those offices. There was always someone laughing, or a team having a discussion about the previous evening's television offerings.

But *Honey* was a small office, and when something big was going on, it affected everyone. It was impossible to avoid.

"Chloe?"

She jumped. Helen was suddenly beside her and sitting down on the corner of her desk. All Chloe could see was a thigh as Helen's skirt slit parted. She knew she shouldn't be looking, but she couldn't help it.

A hundred thoughts clattered through her brain. How had Helen crept up on her? Was she about to be fired? Why couldn't she tear her eyes away from that toned thigh? Why was she describing the thigh as toned? And why was she *still* looking at it?

She dragged her eyes up to Helen's face. Luckily, Helen was looking at her mobile phone screen.

"Yes?"

"This podcast, it's run by a friend of yours, right?" Helen looked away from the phone and down at Chloe.

Chloe swallowed. "Friendish. We, we went to university together. I don't really know her. I—"

"Do you think you can speak to her and get me on the podcast?" Helen interrupted.

"You? Um. S-sure, I can ask. I, you mean, you want to be interviewed?" She could smell Helen's perfume. It felt like the sweet smell was turning her brain upside down.

"That's right. As soon as possible."

Those glasses make her look so hot, Chloe's brain supplied. She coughed and tore her eyes away from Helen.

"I can text her?" she suggested. It came out almost as a squeak.

"You do that. I'll wait to see what she says."

Chloe picked up her phone in a shaky hand. Thankfully, Helen went back to looking at her own phone. She started to draft a quick message to Donna. Her mind kept wandering to Helen's petite frame as it sat on the edge of her desk.

Plenty of people perched on the edge of desks. Kim did it a lot. Chloe herself did it. It shouldn't have been a big deal, but Chloe couldn't stop thinking about it. Her breath was catching in her throat at the very idea of having Helen so close to her. She swore she could feel the heat radiating from Helen's body.

Thankfully, Donna replied quickly, probably salivating at the prospect of getting the editor of *Honey* on her show.

"She, um, wants to know when you're free?" Chloe asked.

"As soon as possible," Helen repeated without looking up from her phone.

Chloe relayed the message and waited. Three dots appeared immediately as Donna formulated a reply.

Helen crossed her legs. Chloe bit her lip. Why did these things happen to her? Why did she get these ridiculous crushes that rendered her useless? This was supposed to be a fun crush, one where she could appreciate Helen from afar and not become so enamoured that she couldn't even speak. But she'd somehow skidded right past an appropriate crush and into a melted puddle of uselessness.

Donna's reply came back fast.

"Tonight?" Chloe asked.

"That's perfect. Can you set it up?" Helen asked, not looking up.

"Sure," Chloe agreed.

"And you'll be coming with me." Helen stood.

"M-me?"

"Yes, you. She's your contact. And I don't know where

her office… house… whatever is." With that, Helen walked away.

Chloe watched her leave. So much for a quiet evening of gorging on pizza followed by an early night. Now, she'd have to take Helen to see Donna and try not to let her out-of-control crush be too visible. How she was going to do that, she had no idea.

"I hope Helen gets some talking points from Fiona for this," Natasha mumbled, clearly having overheard everything.

Chloe shrugged. She didn't know what Helen planned, and she had no intention of getting involved.

CHAPTER THIRTY-FOUR

AN INTERNAL CALL lit up Kim's phone. It was Wendy.

"Hey," Kim answered.

"Hi, could you do me a favour?" Wendy asked.

"Sure, what's up?"

"I need to leave early, one of the kids is unwell. Could you woman reception for me?"

Kim smirked at Wendy's tendency to gender-bend masculine terms. "*Woman* the desk?"

"Yes, look after it, love it. Don't leave it on the bus or give it ice cream before bed," Wendy joked.

"Sure, I can do all that. Hope the sprog is okay."

"Thanks, love. I'm dashing out now, see you tomorrow."

Kim put the phone down and gathered her things together. She stood up and knocked on Helen's door.

"I'm going to sit in reception, Wendy's had to head out."

Helen nodded. She ran a casual ship. No one had to sign in or out, no one was closely monitored. Helen gave people space and respect and expected them to get on with their jobs without being micromanaged.

It was one of the things that had drawn Kim to *Honey* and had kept her there. Of course, she liked her job and loved working for Helen. But it was the trust that had been absent in other workplaces that she really enjoyed. No one looked at their watch and raised a sarcastic eyebrow if she was two minutes late to work.

Well, Pippa tried. But everyone ignored her.

If Kim did leave *Honey*, she wondered if she'd be able to find another workplace that was so laid-back. Not that she wanted to leave, but the prospect of being at *Honey* without Lucy was hard to consider. And the idea that Helen would find out and their working relationship would become strained was a heavy weight on Kim's shoulders.

She settled down at Wendy's desk, moving the crocheted Wonder Woman doll to one side. Wendy's area was more domain than desk. Underneath were shoes, boots, three umbrellas, and several stacks of paperwork. To the side was a large paper bag with knitting needles and wool sticking out of the top.

If *Honey* did close, they'd need to hire a man and a van to get Wendy's belongings to her house.

"Wendy, you've changed," Lucy joked as she stepped back into the office.

"Yeah, thought I'd try life as a black woman in her twenties. You like?" Kim gestured to her face.

"I like a lot." Lucy grinned.

Kim bit her lip and looked into the main office to check they were alone. She waved her hand to get Lucy to come closer. They'd hardly had any time to talk lately, and she needed to let her know about the Pippa incident.

"What's up?" Lucy walked around the desk and perched on top of a low filing cabinet, out of sight of the rest of the office.

"Pippa."

Lucy rolled her eyes. "Isn't she always? What has she said now?"

"She has a friend, if you can believe that, at one of the companies you applied to work for. They told her that you told them that you thought you might be made redundant. Pippa accused me of sharing confidential information."

Lucy's hand shot to her mouth. "Shit," she mumbled.

Kim waved her concerns away. "Tess took the fall for me. She said that she'd overheard something, and she told you. Of course, Pippa doesn't want to get Tess in trouble. No one else will work with her. So, she agreed to keep quiet. But I wanted you to know, just in case."

"I'm so sorry." Lucy lowered her hand to her lap. "I… I didn't think it would get out. I wanted to be honest when people asked why I was leaving. People always assume the worst, so I thought saying I'd heard a rumour about downsizing was the best thing to do. In hindsight, maybe it wasn't."

"It's okay, I just wanted you to know what had been said." Kim leaned in her chair to check they were still alone. "We need to stick to the same story, you know?"

"Bloody Pippa." Lucy's hands clenched in her lap. "I can't believe she accused you of that."

"Well, she wasn't wrong," Kim reminded her. "We can't be angry that someone worked out the truth."

Lucy blew out a sigh. "I hate lying."

"Me too," Kim agreed. "And I hate the idea of being here without you."

Lucy reached out her hand. Kim took it in hers and squeezed it.

"I'll miss you, too. It will be so weird not working together every day," Lucy said.

Kim retracted her hand. "I'm thinking of leaving, too."

Lucy's eyes widened. "What? You love it here!"

"It will be different without you. And I can hardly look Helen in the eye." She put her elbow on the armrest and tilted her head into her hand. "And I don't know if you noticed, but *Honey*'s kinda sucky at the moment."

Lucy smiled sadly. "Yeah, it is. But don't give up a safe, well-paying job without giving it a lot of thought. The market is pretty quiet at the moment. In fact, I'm freaking out about it."

Kim wheeled her chair closer and put her hand on Lucy's leg. "It will be okay, something will turn up."

"Oh, there are *some* jobs. They just come with a much lower salary than what I'm earning here. And I don't know how much time I have. If I have to take the first job I'm offered, it's probably going to be a big salary cut. If I had more time to shop around and pick the right job, it would be a different story. But I don't. Or, at least, I don't think I do."

Kim knew that Lucy was worried about money. Living in London was expensive. And Lucy didn't have a safety net. No savings, no family.

"Move in with me," Kim suggested.

Lucy's mouth fell open in shock. It had only been three months of dating, after all.

"We're at each other's places all the time anyway," Kim pressed on. "I know it's really early—I'm not saying we get married or anything. Just… live together. Or, I'll move in with you. But your place is tiny. Anyway, that would help with your salary problems. You can even put some money aside for your savings account, which you have been talking about for ages."

"Kim," Lucy said.

"And I'll cook," she continued so that Lucy couldn't say no. "As long as you clean. Because I don't dust, I hoover dust up and you don't like that. So, you can dust."

"Kim," Lucy repeated.

"It's too soon, I know."

Lucy put her hand over Kim's mouth. "Kim. I'm trying to say yes. I'd love to move in together."

Kim jumped to her feet and pulled Lucy into a hug.

Lucy wrapped her arms around her and held her tight. "You're such a goof," she mumbled in her ear.

"Hey, I was trying to justify what looks like a really knee-jerk reaction," Kim said.

"My goof," Lucy said.

"Fine, I'm a goof, as long as I'm a goof who is living with her girlfriend."

"Is everything okay?"

They both pulled apart at the sound of Fiona's voice. She looked at them curiously, the reception door closing behind her. Kim considered that maybe she'd picked the wrong location to have the conversation.

"Everything's great." Lucy wiped a tear from her cheek and smiled. "We're moving in together."

Fiona smiled, looking genuinely happy for them. "That's wonderful news! Congratulations. We need some good news today."

"How did things go with Nicola?" Kim asked. "Wendy said you'd spoken to her?"

A hint of a blush crept onto Fiona's cheeks, probably still embarrassed about her outburst that had caused Nicola to quit.

"Quite well, I think she's coming back."

And Kim had thought she couldn't be shocked anymore. "That's great news! Helen will be pleased; do you want to tell her or should I?"

"I'll drop her an email," Fiona said. "Speaking of which, I better get back to it. Congratulations again."

"Thanks," Lucy said.

Fiona walked into the office, and Kim let out a sigh of relief.

"I hope she's managed to convince Nicola to come back, that would really help," she said. "Did you know how expensive photographers and stock photography is? I didn't. Helen's had me looking into it."

"Hey, no talking about work already." Lucy nudged her playfully. "Let's enjoy the fact that we're moving in together first."

Kim's cheeks ached from the smile she couldn't get under control.

Darcy walked into reception. "Lucy, there's a call for you, they said it was important and they'd hold." She looked between the two of them. "What's going on? Why are you smiling?"

Lucy kissed Kim's cheek. "You tell her, I'll grab this call." She hurried away into the office.

"We're moving in together," Kim told Darcy.

Darcy clapped her hands together quickly. "Yay, that's great news!"

"It's not too soon, is it?"

Darcy shrugged. "I don't know, only you two can answer that. But I think it's great news."

Kim nodded quickly. "It is pretty great, isn't it? I was sure she'd say no."

Darcy's smile was huge. Too big for someone who had just come from the marketing department on the day when the company was falling down around their ears.

"You look suspiciously happy," Kim said.

"I'm happy for you," Darcy claimed.

"Try again," Kim suggested.

Darcy's grin got impossibly wiser. "Celia knows who I am. Helen introduced me. And I said something smart, like, really smart."

Kim held her hand up in the air. "I request the highest of fives."

Darcy walked up to her and smacked her hand against Kim's.

"Way to go," Kim congratulated her. "We need to celebrate after work. You, me, Lucy, and Rose. Drinks!"

"What about Chloe?" Darcy asked.

Kim laughed. "She's out with Helen, saving the company. I'll tell you all about it over drinks. Just be glad it's not you!"

CHAPTER THIRTY-FIVE

DESPITE THE LOUD rumbling of the train, Chloe held her breath. It was part of her new plan to sink into the train seat and vanish into nothing. If she held her breath and didn't move a muscle, there was perhaps a chance that Helen wouldn't notice her. Maybe, if she was very lucky, Helen would forget she existed and go hire a new digital assistant.

Not that Chloe no longer wanted to work at *Honey*. She just didn't want to be thought of as the troublemaker who brought the company to its knees. In her first week.

She cast a glance at the woman sitting beside her. Helen hadn't said much since they left the office.

As they stepped onto the street, Helen had asked the address of where they were going. Chloe told her, and Helen quickly calculated the best route to get there. Following a confirmation of her travel plans with Chloe, she flagged a black cab down and instructed the driver to take them to Charing Cross Station, so they could get an overground train.

Since then, Helen's attention had been consumed by her phone. Which Chloe was eternally grateful for. She didn't have much to say to Helen. She wanted to apologise more, but she knew it wouldn't be well received. And she couldn't exactly make small talk with the boss of the company, she had no idea what to say.

Silence was best all round.

"Sorry for having my nose in my phone," Helen said without looking up.

Jinxed it, Chloe thought.

"It's fine." Her eyes snapped to the back of the seat in front of her. "You're a busy person."

Helen chuckled bitterly. "I am." She let out a breath and lowered her phone to her lap. She looked out of the window at the passing scenery. "That doesn't stop my ex from trying to sue me for everything I have."

Chloe swallowed nervously. She'd known about Helen's divorce from day one, it wasn't exactly a secret within the office. But she still didn't quite feel comfortable speaking about it.

If she couldn't make small talk with Helen without making herself sound like an idiot, then this was definitely beyond her area of expertise.

"I'm sorry."

Helen distractedly waved her hand. "Don't worry. I shouldn't have mentioned it. It just frustrates me, we were so close and now—see, I'm doing again. I'm sorry, I don't mean to make you uncomfortable."

"I'm not uncomfortable," Chloe said.

It was a lie. She was deeply uncomfortable. If she had been holding her breath before, now she was practically turning blue. The very idea of having a conversation with Helen about her impending divorce filled her with dread.

But Helen had brought it up. With someone she hardly knew, which probably meant she needed to talk about it. Chloe would have to put her discomfort to one side and do the right thing and be there for her. And try her best to not say something stupid, like telling her that her non-existent door was always open.

"It's fine," Chloe added. "Feel free to… vent."

Helen leaned her head against the window of the train. Her hand clenched around the mobile phone resting on her lap.

"You never think that divorce will happen to you," she began. "You think it's one of those things that happens to other people. People who probably weren't well-suited to begin with. Relationships people set a stopwatch for at the beginning. We were never like that, we were close, we worked." Helen sighed.

Chloe knew she had two choices.

Sadly, silence wasn't one of them.

She could either nod and agree and hope the conversation would be over as quickly humanly possible. Or she could actually engage in conversation, try to be of some use. The former was easier, the latter was more her style. Chloe was always there for her friends. While Helen certainly wasn't her friend, more her tremendously impressive and beautiful boss, Chloe still felt a pull to try to help with the obvious emotional stress that she was going through.

It may have been a ridiculous decision, but Chloe couldn't help herself as she hurtled towards certain disaster.

"I'm really sorry you're getting a divorce. I don't know

much about it, but I can imagine it's very emotionally draining and hard to deal with."

After offering up those words, she waited with baited breath.

The ball was in Helen's court now. She could brush off Chloe's comments, quickly returning them to the boss/employee relationship. Or, just maybe, she might start a conversation. Chloe didn't know which she'd prefer.

"It *is* very emotionally draining," Helen agreed. "I think the suddenness of it is what I struggle with most. I didn't even know we were in trouble. Isn't that strange?" She turned to face Chloe.

Chloe could see sadness in her eyes. And for one brief, terrifying moment she wondered if Helen would cry.

"It was sudden?" Chloe asked tentatively. She was reminded of her own relationship ending, though that had been anything but sudden. More a long, drawn-out death that she wished she had had the courage to euthanise sooner. Not that she had identified that at the time. At the time, she had thought she was happy. It was only when it had all fallen apart that she had finally realised how unhappy she had been.

"Very," Helen said. "Quite unknown to me, she was having an affair with a *child*."

Chloe couldn't help the gasp that escaped her lips.

"An affair?" She knew she sounded angry. She was angry. How could anyone do that to Helen? Okay, she didn't know her that well, but she couldn't imagine why anyone would do something like that in general—*especially* not to Helen, who seemed so amazing.

If she was ever lucky enough to be in a relationship

with someone as great her boss, she'd do everything to make it work. But she knew that there were sometimes things that went on behind closed doors. Even so, for some reason, she couldn't see Helen as the villain of this story.

A soft smile formed on Helen's lips. She nodded. "Yes, an affair. I call my replacement the high schooler."

"Are they still together?" Chloe asked. Any notion of not engaging in the conversation had flown right out of the sealed train windows. She was now fully invested.

"Oh yes, very much so. Blissfully happy if what I'm led to believe is correct." Helen turned to look out of the window again. "And now they want everything. The house, most of the cash, the cottage, the car, of course, she always loved that car. And I'll be left with, well, nothing. Well, my health. Because, apparently, I should be wildly grateful for the fact that I still have my health, if my mother is to be believed."

"That's terrible," Chloe said. "I mean… all of it. I can't believe that your ex wants to take everything. And that your mother wasn't more sympathetic. I mean, yes, it's great that you have your health. But that doesn't counteract everything else."

"Oh, my mother doesn't do sympathy. She's a very pragmatic woman," Helen said.

Pragmatic, Chloe thought. *That isn't my take on it.*

"It still sounds terrible," she mumbled.

Helen turned to her, a small smile on her face. She looked at Chloe as if she thought she was naïve, innocent; basically, not in the real world. Chloe had seen the look before from many of her friends and even her family. It wasn't that she didn't know how the world worked, she just wanted to actively try to be different from it.

"It *is* terrible," Helen agreed. "But it's life. And, of course, I'll be taking her to court and attempting to keep everything."

"How can she even think she has a claim on those things?" Chloe asked. The moment the words passed her lips, she wondered if perhaps she had gone too far. She was so interested that she had forgot to put the stops on her rampant curiosity, the same trait that sometimes got her into trouble.

But Helen casually shrugged a shoulder.

"We've been together, I mean we *had been* together, a long time. She was with me long before any of this, before *Honey*, before I was anything. Her father is a divorce lawyer. Something I should have considered before marrying her. Anyone who grew up listening to tales of divorce, broken marriage, and the distribution of wealth is going to have a warped sense of right and wrong. Anyway, he is, of course, dealing with the case. And, of course, he has never liked me. I think he believes that I turned his sweet and innocent girl into a lesbian."

Helen's eyes sparkled with mischief. Chloe wondered for a brief second if it had been true. She was fairly convinced that Helen could make anyone rethink their sexuality. There was something so powerful, enigmatic, and attractive about her personality. And that was before you even got to the fact that she was drop-dead gorgeous.

"I don't think it's right, that she thinks she can take everything," Chloe said.

"No, you're right. It isn't. And she shouldn't be able to

do that. But she can. Well, she's going to try. She has the high schooler whispering in her ear, at least that's what I tell myself. The alternative is that she hates me so much she would gladly see me destitute." Helen shook her head and turned away. "As much as I hate her, I can't believe that this is all her own will. I have to believe that someone else is trying to convince her that this is the best course of action."

Chloe's heart clenched. When she had waded into the conversation, she had never considered how it would feel to hear Helen in so much pain. The stray smile, the odd chuckle, none of it amounted to much. Helen was clearly a woman in distress, her life falling down around her.

It made Chloe want to do something to help. She wanted to take Helen into her arms and whisper into her hair that she would make it all better. She wanted to rush to the rescue and take all the pain away. Even though she knew she couldn't. She was nothing to Helen. Just an employee. One who had badly messed up and was now adding more to Helen's overfilled plate.

"I'm really sorry," Chloe said. "For everything. But mainly for causing so much stress with this stupid podcast. I didn't mean to cause all this trouble. I wish I could turn back time and not do it. I know it triggered a lot of problems for *Honey*, but I'm mainly sorry about the extra stress that it caused you."

Helen continued to look out the window. Chloe wondered if she was hiding her face from her. She'd be devastated if she'd made her cry.

"I, I know the end of relationships can be hard," Chloe said. "I recently came out of a long-term relationship.

Nothing like a divorce, I know. But we had been together for five years."

Helen turned to face her, an eyebrow raised in curiosity. "That is a long time."

"Yeah. It ended about six months ago, I'm still not properly over it. I mean, I don't want her back, I wasn't happy. But it's hard when your life is turned upside down. I'm sure you feel the same way."

"I do," Helen agreed. "Why did you break up, if you don't mind me asking? Feel free to not tell me. I'm not asking as your boss."

I woke up, Chloe thought. She didn't dare say that, she didn't want Helen to think she was weak.

"We… wanted different things. We'd been arguing a lot, for a long time." Chloe blew out a breath. How did you summarise a twelve-month breakup in a few short sentences? "She gave me ultimatums, eventually I'd had enough. I didn't want to live like that anymore."

"Sounds rough."

"It was," Chloe agreed. "Very. And then after was bad for me as well. I had no money, so I had to move in with my parents. It was nice of them to take me in, but it was so embarrassing. I know people think I'm young, but I'm an independent adult and to have to go back to Mum and Dad… it was demeaning."

"I can imagine," Helen commiserated. "On one hand, it's nice to have the option. On the other, you don't want to appear—"

"Like you messed up your life," Chloe finished.

Helen opened her mouth. Her expression said that she was about to disagree.

"No, it's true. I got into a relationship that wasn't healthy for me. I stayed too long. And I gave up a lot of my independence, and, because I did that, I lost all of it in the end." Chloe shook her head at her behaviour. "My dad has always viewed me as his little girl. In some respects, he thinks I can run the world, in others he thinks I can't cross the road by myself. This whole thing really didn't help. He's started treating me like I'm twelve again."

Helen chuckled. "Well, allow me to tell you that there's no age limit on life-altering breakups. You can be eighteen or eighty, we all make the same mistakes at some point. I'm sure your parents care about you deeply and don't want to see you hurt. I doubt they see you as any less of an adult now as a result of what happened."

Chloe hummed noncommittally. Helen hadn't met Chloe's parents. Thank goodness.

"I'm just relieved I never had kids," Helen said. "That would be another horrible complication in this mess. Well, we didn't birth any kids. She obviously has one now, what with high schooler."

Chloe grinned. "How old is the interloper?"

"Nineteen."

Chloe's eyebrows shot up. She let out a low whistle. "And your ex is?"

"Thirty-six. I thought our age gap was rather large, but she almost doubled it."

Chloe knew there was a clue in there to working out Helen's age. She'd already ascertained that Helen was in her mid-forties. Her brain swam with the information, but she was too exhausted to figure out the puzzle.

"I'm sorry for your breakup," Helen said earnestly.

"And I'm sorry for yours," Chloe replied. "And the whole podcast thing. Really, if I could take it back, I would."

Helen let go of her phone and placed a hand on Chloe's thigh, close to her knee. She gave the briefest of pats before removing her hand again. It was an innocent gesture, but one that sent Chloe's temperature is skyrocketing.

"Don't worry," Helen commanded softly. "I'll fix it. I always do."

The conversation was over. Chloe didn't know how she felt about it. On the one hand, she was back to wanting to disappear into the cushion seat, vanish from existence to eradicate the awkwardness she felt. On the other, she'd just had a deep and meaningful conversation with Helen.

Which of course meant that her crush was now fully out of control. She wished it wasn't the case, but Chloe rarely had any say in how her crushes developed. What Helen Featherstone didn't know was that she was slowly becoming an important component to Chloe's world. And the fact that she had personally caused her trouble and pain made her feel worse than the potential collapse of *Honey Magazine*.

I'm doomed, Chloe thought.

CHAPTER THIRTY-SIX

THE COUNTRY'S biggest lesbian culture podcast was operated out of a shed in Donna Hayward's parents' back garden. Chloe had seen it the day before, but Helen hadn't been aware. She looked bemused as she was let down the garden path, nodding politely at Donna's parents before entering the shed.

Chloe was hoping to be able to stay away from the whole thing, but Helen had other ideas, wanting her to be close by. Chloe had agreed but had decided to stay far, far away from the microphones. She didn't want a repeat of the day before. If Pippa wanted her blood now, she'd also add a pound of flesh to her shopping list if Chloe was allowed to speak on air again.

Chloe sat in the corner of the admittedly large shed. She watched as Donna conducted her various soundtracks, clearly excited to have someone like Helen on the show.

Helen sat primly at the desk, her hands folded neatly on her lap as she waited for Donna to be ready.

Chloe couldn't believe how calm she appeared. It had just been twenty minutes earlier that they had been discussing the horrors of her divorce. She guessed that was why Helen was the boss: professionalism. The ability to compartmentalise the failure of her relationship and focus on the recovery of her business. However she intended to do that. Chloe still had no idea what Helen's plans were. No clue what she intended to say to the listening public, how she going to fix Chloe's terrible mess.

Donna finished the final sound check. She swung the microphone into position above her head and pinned Helen with a smile.

Jealousy shot straight through Chloe like lightning rolling over a countryside. She hated that Donna had the opportunity to even lay her deceiving eyes on someone as pure as Helen.

She had spent most of the day trying to ignore the whole podcast debacle, but the silence of the office had made it impossible. There was no distraction, nothing to think about other than what she had heard on the playback of the show. During the course of the day, she'd become painfully aware of the fact that Donna had shafted her. And the worst thing, she had no idea why.

"Right," Donna said. "I'm ready if you are?"

Helen leaned forward, reached up, and pulled her microphone towards her.

"I'm ready. I would just like to insist going in that I have final say on any edits." Helen smiled politely. Her tone sounded neutral enough, but it was clear that she was issuing a command, showing her authority over Donna.

"The show goes out tonight. I don't know if I would have time," Donna said.

Helen pushed herself back from the desk and stood up. "If that's the case, I can't possibly engage in an interview. My legal team would never allow it. As a professional, I'm sure you understand?"

Donna stood up as well. Panic was clear in her eyes. "Absolutely, we're both professionals, I'm sure we can figure something out," she appealed.

Chloe couldn't blame her. This was probably the interview of her career. While the podcast had many listeners, it hadn't quite broken through to booking celebrities. With the likes of the editor-in-chief of *Honey Magazine*, it could be a stepping stone that Donna was clearly eager to get on.

"How about we do this in one take?" Helen suggested. "I'm sure a professional such as yourself can manage that? If you agree to broadcast the show exactly as it happens, then I'll be happy to proceed. However, if I later find out that the interview has been edited in any way, I will potentially have to seek legal advice. I'm sure you'll understand?"

"Absolutely," Donna said. "I completely agree. And that sounds absolutely fine. I'm sure, between the both of us, we can manage. Aside from topping and tailing the show with the standard marketing messages, there won't be a need to edit."

"Wonderful." Helen sat down again. "Of course, we'll stay to see the final version of the show be uploaded."

Chloe's stomach growled at the thought. It was going to be a long night.

"You're more than welcome to stay," Donna confirmed.

"Wonderful. Let's begin."

Donna went through some housekeeping. It was exactly the same exact speech she had given Chloe the day before. Chloe bit down on her cheek at the memory. She'd been so excited, so eager to help *Honey*, that she'd walked right into Donna's well-placed trap.

She wanted to turn the equipment off, grab Donna by her T-shirt, and pull her to her feet. She wanted to demand to know why Donna had conned her. To ask what she had ever done to her.

Donna started the show. She introduced Helen, carefully avoiding mentioning anything to do with *Honey's* financial difficulties which had been so centre stage in her previous show. Chloe wondered if Donna was perhaps a little frightened of Helen or just respectful of how useful an ally she could be.

"Thank you, Donna," Helen said. "It's a delight to be on the show."

"You're welcome, it's great to have you here. I was wondering—"

"If I may," Helen interrupted, "I'd like to address a couple of issues that were brought up on your show yesterday."

The phrasing gave Donna little opportunity to say no. "Yes, of course."

"I just wanted to say that Chloe Dixon, whom you spoke to yesterday, was slightly misquoted."

Slightly? Chloe thought. *That's being generous.*

"I'm not sure why," Helen said with a small chuckle, "but it came across as if *Honey* was in financial difficulty. And I simply must put a stop to those rumours. *Honey* is nowhere near closing the doors. We are a successful, buoyant company, and any rumours of cashflow issues are grossly exaggerated. As the editor-in-chief, I can tell you with my hand on my heart that our balance sheet is sturdy."

"Would it be accurate to say that *Honey* is struggling?" Donna fished.

"Oh, absolutely," Helen said.

Chloe's head snapped up. She stared at Helen, wondering if she'd gone mad. Or if she was leading into some kind of joke.

"As is every other magazine probably in the world," Helen continued. "Print is a dated medium, as is the act of paying for great quality content. But I have to say that the magazine industry has never been an easy one. I don't think you'll find a single editor who would ever say that it's easy. And that's one of the reasons why I love the industry, and *Honey* in particular, so much.

"I do fear," Helen admitted, "where things are going. Subscriptions are down across the board for magazines, and *Honey* is not immune. I think that's a shame, not just because I am in charge and because it provides me with my livelihood, but because *Honey* is special. *Honey* is something unique in our world. But I think that maybe people have taken it for granted. That they assume it will always be there. But the truth is, it might not be.

"I think, and I'm sure you'll agree, Donna, with more LBT women than ever being out it's important to have an outlet dedicated to us, to our culture, to our interests, to our community. *Honey Magazine* isn't just about saying we love women, it's so much more than that. The magazine promotes movies, TV shows, books, and albums. Every-thing created by people within our community. It's with that insight into the community, what we produce, what we consume, that we, as a community, will continue to grow. And not be ignored. I worry that with the general trend of magazine distribution shrinking, magazines like *Honey* will lose the opportunity to be a showcase for our pooled talents. We need a voice. And I don't just say that as the editor of a magazine. I say that as a lesbian woman. As someone who grew up wondering why I was different, and if I would ever, ever find someone else like me in the world.

"Well, I did, and it was glorious. I think everyone in our situation will remember a time when they felt utterly alone. A time when they felt like no one else was like them. And if *Honey* can reach out to just *one* person and say to them 'you're not alone,' then I feel it's worth fighting for. And I've had a successful day at work."

It took everything within Chloe to not stand up and applaud. It was everything that she had ever thought about *Honey Magazine*, and her community as a whole.

She didn't believe in walls that separated people, but she did believe in safe spaces where people could experience their own culture without having to fight through all the mainstream noise.

Helen got that. Helen understood exactly how Chloe, and many thousands of other women, were feeling.

Chloe's chest expanded with pride. Even to just be the person who led Helen to Donna Hayward's parents' shed at the bottom of a garden in Greater London. It was a small thing, one she had no say in, but she'd been a small part of allowing people to hear Helen speak.

Even Donna seemed shaken. She blinked a couple of times, seemingly gathering her thoughts.

"You're right. You're absolutely right. That is one of the reasons why I set up the podcast. We need representation, we need content for our corner of the world," Donna said, her head vigorously nodding.

"Absolutely, I'm glad we agree. I would love nothing more an explosion of LBT media, and that includes podcasts, magazines, movies, television, books, anything you can imagine. I want there to be as much LBT content as humanly possible. I want to show the world what we can produce, how incredible it is. And not just for us. It's for everyone to see.

"When LBT producers come up with a fantastic movie, I want to use our community to springboard that movie into the spotlight. *Honey Magazine*, and other outlets, are the stepping stone, the springboard, to showcasing our talent to the world."

"Yes! Exactly!" Donna was excited now. She sat forward in her chair, eagerly nodding her agreement with Helen's words. "There is no reason why our content shouldn't be front and centre with the rest of the world's mainstream content."

"Of course not, but it's a crowded market space," Helen said. "With innovations in technology, so many people are able to create independent movies, albums, books, plays—anything, really. That makes for a very busy marketplace, lots and lots of content. We need our media spaces in order to showcase *our* content. Picking up a copy of *Honey Magazine* isn't a political statement, it's not a dating magazine. It's so much more than that. It's curated content about our community, showcasing our talent. It's essential work, I'm sure you'll agree, Donna. After all, we are in the same business."

Donna continued nodding like an excited puppy ready for its first walk.

"We are, we really are."

"I believe," Helen said, "that having a publication like *Honey* is as important now as it was when it launched twenty-four years ago. But maybe I'm wrong."

Chloe stared at Helen. She wondered what she was about to say. A chill ran up her spine. Of course, Helen wasn't wrong. Chloe couldn't even begin to fathom that she was. Everything that Helen had just said had been nothing short of a masterstroke of genius. She spoke with such passion and determination. Chloe would have loved to have been able to articulate her feelings in such a powerful way.

"If subscriber numbers continue to drop," Helen said, "then I'm wrong. And *Honey* isn't relevant anymore."

Even Donna looked dumbstruck at the very idea. Somehow, Helen had managed to get Donna to perform a complete one-eighty. From trying to bring *Honey* down around Chloe's ears to suddenly looking almost distraught at the idea of that happening. Visibly upset at the notion of *Honey* being irrelevant.

"I hope I'm wrong," Helen said. "I hope that people continue to find *Honey* as relevant, exciting, innovative, and interesting as it has always been. But the proof will be in the sales figures. We strive to produce the best-quality magazine we can, we do extensive market research to ensure that what we are putting into the magazine is what our readers want. That's the best we can do: produce the best we can. If people don't pick it up, then maybe I am wrong and maybe *Honey* is irrelevant in today's modern society. Time will tell."

Understanding washed over Chloe. It was a call to arms. It was masterfully done, subtle but somehow honest and from the heart.

Donna's brow was furrowed. She looked at Helen like someone who had found a kindred spirit, maybe even a leader.

"I really could not have said it better myself," she said. "Everything you've just said hits the nail right on the head, and that's why we need to support our LBT spaces. We fought to have these things, we need to ensure we continue to support them."

Donna was on board, and Chloe was left to wonder what on earth she had done to offend her so much the previous day.

The interview continued on. Donna asked questions and Helen answered them. There was a friendliness that had been missing from the day before. Things seemed lighter, and the future appeared brighter.

Chloe tuned out. She was too busy looking at Helen. She sat stone still, staring at the woman who had just given such an impassioned speech. It was everything Chloe felt and more. She knew she was looking at her new hero.

If Donna's audience was rallied enough and started to pick up copies of *Honey*, maybe even to subscribe, then perhaps things would be okay. Hopefully, the business would be saved.

And maybe Chloe could convince herself that doing the podcast in the first place wasn't a huge mistake. Okay, so she'd needed Helen's help. But they never would have had the opportunity without Chloe contacting Donna to start with.

But all of that faded into the background. Because now Chloe had a new problem. She was no longer concerned about the fact she had nearly brought down *Honey* in her first week. She was worried about the fact that her out-of-control crush on Helen Featherstone had quickly developed into full-on hero worship.

Maybe she did need to look for a new job after all.

CHAPTER THIRTY-SEVEN

"So, how was I?" Helen asked.

Amazing, incredible, unbelievable, awe-inspiring, Chloe thought.

"Good," she said. "I mean really good."

There was a very fine line between trying to keep her crush a secret and sounding like she was unimpressed. A fine line that Chloe struggled to walk.

Helen nodded. She had seemed deep in thought ever since they had started up the quiet, residential street towards the local station to get their respective trains home.

"I think it will help," Chloe added, realising she needed to say something else.

"I hope so. It is true that *Honey* isn't *quite* destitute yet, but we are in trouble. And I meant what I said, I do think *Honey* is an important vehicle for our community. And the salary is quite nice, too."

Chloe chuckled at the joke. She was about to reply when her mobile phone rang. She got her phone out of her bag and saw that it was her parents. Or at least one of them.

"I'm sorry, I have to get this."

"Of course, you're not technically at work anymore," Helen commented.

Chloe answered the call. "Hello?"

"Hello, it's me," Mum said loudly. She was on loudspeaker, so of course she was shouting at the top of her lungs. Chloe suspected that Helen could hear her, if the small smirk on her face was anything to go by.

"Hi Mum," Chloe greeted. "Is everything okay?"

"Yes, I'm just checking if you like broccoli?"

Chloe's cheeks flushed with heat.

"Well, no, not really," she admitted in a small voice. There was something devastating about admitting to disliking broccoli in front of your very sexy boss.

Helen tutted softly under her breath. Chloe glanced at her. She winked. If it was possible, Chloe's cheeks became hotter, and her heart slammed against her rib cage.

"What about cauliflower?" Mum asked.

"Yeah, that's fine," Chloe said.

"Oh, good, and you're not on any weird health kick at the moment, are you? Like, you can eat gluten? Yes?"

"Yes." Chloe couldn't believe this conversation was happening right now. "No health kick, everything is normal. Anything else?"

"No, just that. I thought you liked broccoli?" Mum questioned.

Chloe wanted to die. She was right back to where she was a couple of hours earlier on the train, wishing to somehow vanish into nothingness. Why did she answer the call? Why did Mum suddenly not recall her vegetable preferences?

"I don't, Mum," Chloe admitted. She hoped that not giving her mother any more fuel would bring the conversation to a speedy end.

She was wrong.

"What is it you don't like about it?" Mum asked.

Helen's shoulders shook as she tried to contain her laughter.

"Can we talk about this later, Mum?" Chloe asked.

"Why?" Her mother wasn't great at catching a hint. Or letting something go.

"Because I'm with someone," Chloe said.

"Who?"

Chloe resisted the urge to throw the phone across the street, watch it shatter, and then continue walking to the train station as if nothing had ever happened.

"My boss," she said.

"The stuck-up one?" Mum asked.

This time Helen did laugh out loud. She looked at Chloe with an amused raised eyebrow.

"I never said she was stuck up, I never said anyone was stuck up," Chloe said into the phone. She looked Helen. "I never said anyone was stuck up," she promised.

"Hmm," Helen said noncommittally, a grin on her face.

Helen seem to be having a great time at Chloe's expense. Chloe was simply relieved that she wasn't angry.

"You said…" Mum began.

"Look, I need to go. Can I talk to you later, Mum?" Chloe said quickly, putting an end to her mum repeating whatever she thought Chloe had said. Things that she no doubt hadn't said at all but that her mother had deciphered from random comments.

"Okay, okay. Oh, by the way, Dad listened to that podcast. That's Donna Hayward, isn't it?"

Chloe frowned. She didn't remember mentioning Donna's name when she spoke to her parents the other night.

"Yes, do you know her?" she asked. It wasn't unusual for her parents to speak about people like they knew them personally when they didn't. Anyone on TV was fair game. You'd think Mum frequently had movie stars around for dinner the way she quoted things they had apparently said. But mentioning Donna Hayward was a bit of a stretch.

"Yes," Mum said, as it was obvious. "Donna."

"Yes, *I* know her name, how do *you* know her?" Chloe asked.

"You were at university with her. When I came to visit you, you were late back from class, and I spoke to her and her cousin. When you got back you introduced me. She seemed quite nice. But not her cousin, Eloise." Mum said the name as if she had a terrible smell under her nose.

Helen stop walking. Chloe stopped, too. She turned and saw that Helen had gone deathly pale.

"I have to go, Mum, I'll call you later." Chloe hung up the call. She took a step towards Helen. "Are you okay?"

"Eloise Hayward," Helen said. "It didn't even occur to me. It's such a common name."

"You know her?"

"The high schooler," Helen breathed. "Donna is my soon-to-be ex-wife's partner's cousin."

Chloe's eyes widened.

"It seems I owe you an apology, Chloe," Helen said, in the quiet of the street. "Donna wasn't after you, she was after me. Clearly, Eloise spoke to her about me, who knows what was said. And then you came along–and with you the opportunity to trash *Honey*. Of course, she took it."

It made sense. Chloe had been trying to come up with a reason why Donna had sabotaged her interview, but with no success. Even in the deepest recesses of her mind she couldn't remember, or even imagine, doing anything that would make Donna hold a grudge for years after.

"I wonder why she didn't do the same today," Helen mused. "I was sat right there, it would have been easy for her to turn the interview around again. But we both just heard the version that's being sent live. And she seemed rather positive. What changed her mind?"

"You did," Chloe said without thinking. "It's because you spoke with such passion, there's no way she could disagree with what you are saying. Anyone would have agreed with you."

The colour started to return to Helen's face. She smiled and tilted her head to the side. "I thought you said I was just *good*?"

"I said very good," Chloe corrected.

"You did," Helen agreed with a smile.

"I think you convinced Donna that we're on the same side."

"Maybe so." Helen shook her head as if to banish bad thoughts. She gestured with her hand to suggest they continue walking. They fell into step, walking side by side, Helen's heels clicking along the footpath as they did.

"So, why don't you like broccoli?" she asked.

"I don't know," Chloe lied.

It smelt like fart, that was the reason. But there was no way she was going to say that to Helen.

"Personally," Helen said, "I can't stand cauliflower. Broccoli, I'll tolerate, but cauliflower is essentially broccoli with none of the taste. Like dead broccoli."

Chloe laughed.

"No way," she argued. "Cauliflower is great. Broccoli just tastes like it's gone off."

"You need cheese in order to make cauliflower at all palatable," Helen said.

"I had a cauliflower steak couple of weeks ago," Chloe said. "It was really nice."

"I pity your taste buds," Helen said. "Are you a vegetarian?"

"No."

"Then why would you ever choose to have a cauliflower steak rather than an actual meat steak? It's just a gimmick. How much was it?"

Chloe laughed. "Expensive, considering it was a slice out the middle of the cauliflower that probably only cost a pound from Tesco."

Helen chuckled. "See? Gimmick."

"True, you've convinced me," Chloe agreed.

She hadn't at all. The cauliflower steak was delicious. Maybe she'd just make it at home instead, though.

"Your mum sounds nice," Helen said.

"Yeah, she is. But she doesn't know when to stop talking, or when she's embarrassing me."

"Well, I had a wonderful time, it was most entertaining."

"Yes, that's what I was worried about," Chloe said.

"Don't worry, your dislike of broccoli is safe with me."

"And your lack of understanding regarding cauliflower is safe with me," Chloe replied.

They fell into a comfortable silence. The residential street was quiet, birds were singing in the trees, and the evening sun was ducking behind the houses. Chloe couldn't have planned a better moment, walking with her gorgeous boss on a warm summer night, sharing a joke.

She soaked it up like a dry sponge, enjoying the carefree interaction. It wasn't something she could get used to, or something she even expected to ever happen again. She knew she'd relive it in her memories. It had been a long time since she'd simply enjoyed someone's company while being madly attracted to that person.

But she knew it wouldn't go anywhere. She wasn't ready. Helen was in the middle of a divorce. Not to mention that Helen wouldn't look twice at her.

"Eloise Hayward," Helen mumbled. "I can't believe she'd stoop that low."

"It's a shit thing to do," Chloe said. A second after the words were out of her mouth she realised what she had said and slapped a hand over her mouth. She looked apologetically at Helen.

Helen laughed loudly. It sounded magical. Rich, velvety tones which Chloe wanted to hear all the time.

"It's fine, feel free. As I said, we're not in the office now. And you're right, it is a shit thing to do. But I think I won, don't you?"

Chloe grinned. "You did, you really did."

CHAPTER THIRTY-EIGHT

KIM LEANT HEAVILY on the glass door leading to the *Honey* office. It started to open, and she practically hung onto it and let it drag her into reception. She rubbed her eyes and let out a giant yawn. Wendy took one look at her and gently laughed.

"Rough night?"

"Yeah," Kim said. She walked over to Wendy's desk and sat in a spare chair. "Lucy and I spent hours talking about where to live. Like, literally, hours. And, I'm sorry to say that there is nowhere in London for us to live." Kim threw her hands up in a defeated gesture.

Wendy raised an eyebrow. "Nowhere, you mean all these people living in apartments, houses, and even house-boats, but there's nowhere for you two to live?"

"Yep."

"What's wrong with where you live now?" Wendy asked.

"It's too small. Well, both our places are too small. I

mean, I've been complaining about how small my place is since I first moved in. And there's no way I could fit Lucy in my tiny apartment as well. It starts getting crowded when I have to get my winter boots out of storage. And having another human being there, as much as I want her there, full time with all her own stuff… it ain't happening." Kim rested her head on the cold metal of the filing cabinet beside Wendy's desk.

She wasn't exaggerating, she was utterly exhausted. When they started researching places to live, they both thought the answer would be there, waiting for them to find it. But, as they continued to look, they realised that every single place they looked at had some kind of issue. Too small, too expensive, too far away from public transport, too close to noisy nightspots, too run-down. There was always something.

"And Lucy's place?" Wendy asked.

"Same problem. Too small. And her landlord isn't very nice. I don't want to live there, he lives in the apartment over the way and he gives me, well, dodgy looks. So, we're looking for something new. But there isn't anything."

"Oh, now, come on." Wendy shuffled some papers and stapled the top before placing the stack of paperwork in her out-tray. "There must be somewhere in London. You can't have discounted *everywhere*."

"We pretty much have," Kim said. "First, we had a debate about where in town we wanted to be. I love being central, but Lucy says she'd prefer to be somewhere a bit farther out, somewhere a bit quieter. But the farther out you go, the more expensive it is to travel into town. Yeah, the price of rent is cheaper, but I don't have enough organs in my body to sell in order to pay for a Travelcard into work."

"Oh yes, cost of travel has been going up and up and up," Wendy sympathised.

"It really has, and it's already nearly too much for us to afford." Kim slumped further down in the chair. "It was meant to be easy, you know? We were going to move in together, everything would be great. But we can't even agree on a place to live. Well, that's not entirely true, there are places we both like, but unless we win the lottery..."

Wendy rearranged some more papers. She looked at Kim over the top of her glasses. It was her trademark motherly *I know better than you, don't worry* look.

"Something will turn up," she said. "It always does. You've only just agreed to moving in with each other. I know you want to hurry and get everything sorted out, just give yourself a little bit of time. The answer will present itself."

"I hope so," Kim said. "I just... I don't want it to be difficult. I know it's early in our relationship, and I really want things to work. I don't want there to be trouble early on."

She didn't want Lucy to get cold feet and back out is what she meant. She didn't have any indication that Lucy would. But it had been a short amount of time and already Kim was finding that the thought of life without Lucy was unbearable. She didn't want there to be any reason for her girlfriend to think it would be easier to be apart.

"When did you start worrying about things so much?" Wendy asked with a smirk. "Where's the Kim Faulkner I know? The one who is so laid-back she's almost asleep?"

Kim laughed. "Well, she's here, and she really is nearly asleep. I wasn't kidding when I said we were up all hours talking about this."

She rubbed her face, thankful she hadn't put any makeup on that morning. Wendy was right, it wasn't like her to worry about stuff. She was always relaxed, chill. She wondered if the environment at *Honey* lately had caused her to become a bit more stressed. That was something she'd have to look at and work on.

"Did you listen to the podcast last night?" Wendy asked.

Kim shook her head. "No, I wanted a nice, quiet, relaxed evening with Lucy. We didn't need the added stress of another podcast. Not that we had a nice, quiet, relaxed evening. We ended up going mad looking at different properties all over London. Did you hear it, though?"

Wendy quickly shook her head. "I don't know how to podcast, it's all a mystery to me. I'd probably quite like them, I've recently gotten into audiobooks, but I have to ask the man at the library to sort it all out on my phone for me."

Kim's jaw dropped. She stared at Wendy.

"What?" Wendy asked.

"You get a man to put audiobooks on your phone? And I thought you were a feminist!"

"I am a feminist," Wendy said. "I also know my limits. If I need something technical doing, I ask one of you girls, or I ask my friend in the library. I had a dripping tap the other week, and I had a plumber come around to fix it. Men have to have their uses, otherwise they'll get upset. We don't want them moping around because women don't need them anymore."

Kim chuckled. "Well, I suppose we'll find out soon enough whether or not it was a success. And if we're in for another horrible day in the office."

"I think this is the longest week there's ever been," Wendy said. "Thank goodness the heat is breaking, we're supposed to have storms tonight. I'm quite looking forward to it. After all of this hot weather, I think I might stand outside in the rain."

The door opened, and Helen walked in. She had her briefcase in one hand, and a light summer jacket resting over her other arm. She looked at Kim, slumped in the chair.

"Rough night?" she asked.

"Yes, but not how you think," Wendy replied on Kim's behalf.

Helen raised an eyebrow towards Kim.

"Trying to find property in London," Kim said.

"Ah, my commiserations," Helen replied. "I know it's early, but can I talk to you?"

"Sure." Kim got to her feet and followed Helen through to her office. All the way she could feel panic rising up inside her.

She knows, she knows, she knows, her mind unhelpfully chanted at her.

Helen walked into her office and gestured for Kim to take a seat. She closed the door behind them and hung her coat on the coatrack. She placed her briefcase on the edge of her desk and sat down.

"I've been sensing something between us is... amiss," Helen started.

Kim attempted to control her breathing, moderate her posture, and look like there was nothing wrong. She was distantly aware that she probably looked like she had recently been murdered and stuffed.

"No, well... no," she stumbled.

"I was wondering if it was something to do with the email from Christine?" Helen said. She turned in her seat and snapped open the brass locks on her briefcase. She pulled out her MacBook and plugged it into the cables that dangled on her desk. "I left it there for you to see. I assume you saw it? Obviously, I can't tell you anything directly, but I would hope that you would have seen it, and maybe... done something with the information you had?"

Helen looked up.

"You knew?" Kim couldn't believe what she was hearing. Not only did Helen know, she had *wanted* Kim to snoop on her email and report back to Lucy what she had seen.

"Of course, we don't have secrets," Helen said. "My life is an open book, and you have access to everything. I'm fully aware that anything that comes into my email box is fair game. And when I saw the email from Christine..." She rolled her eyes. "Well, obviously I can't warn Lucy myself, but I knew you could. And I hope you did. You did? Didn't you?"

Kim slowly inclined her head. "Yes."

"Good, and how is she getting on? Obviously, I can write a letter of reference. I mean, I don't want to lose her, and I'll fight tooth and nail for her. But it's so like Christine to get a bee in her bonnet about something, and then there is little I can do."

"I've been petrified," Kim admitted.

"Why?" Helen looked genuinely confused.

"Because I snooped in your email, I saw something I didn't think I should, then told Lucy. I broke your trust." All of Kim's pent-up emotions tumbled out. "I thought you'd hate me."

Helen stood up, quickly walked around the desk, and pulled Kim to her feet and into a hug.

"I could never hate you, never. I'm sorry, I didn't realise this has been worrying you so much. I thought you knew that I'd assumed you'd read the email. I was going to speak to you about it earlier, but then all of this podcast business happened. I didn't have time to discuss it with you. I'm sorry, I should have made time."

Helen stepped back but kept her hands on Kim's upper arms and looked at her intently.

"I'm sorry. I feel terrible, I felt like I was spying." Kim sniffled. She felt ridiculous for practically crying in her boss's office, but she couldn't help herself. Everything had built up to a crescendo and come tumbling out.

"But it's your job to manage my email," Helen said, still clearly confused.

"I know, I…" Kim didn't really understand why she had felt the way she did, but she was relieved now. "I just felt bad."

"Well, there's no need. It's all out in the open now. I know you know that I know… and all that. As I say, I'll fight to keep Lucy, really I will. But I can't control Christine, it's like trying to predict a lightning strike."

There was a knock on the office door.

"Come in," Helen called out.

Lucy opened the door. She looked from Kim to Helen with a confused raised eyebrow. Kim wanted to explain to her, to tell her that everything was okay, but she was still struggling to pull herself together. She didn't want to outright burst into tears, and at the moment, as exhausted as she was, it was a close call.

"I just wanted to say," Lucy said when it was clear that neither of them was going to explain what she'd stepped into, "that my phone has been ringing off the hook. We didn't listen to the podcast last night, but whatever you did, it worked. I have so many people wanting to book ad space, but I think we're going to be full for the month. Even the extra pages. And no discounts, nobody even asked, and I haven't offered."

Kim felt ecstatic. She wanted to run over and hug Lucy, which wasn't exactly business appropriate, but she found she didn't care. She quickly pulled her girlfriend into a big bear hug.

She turned to Helen. "What did you say?"

"The truth," her boss answered. "Apparently, there is still an appetite for it. And it seems we won't be needing to look into outsourcing our advertising after all."

CHAPTER THIRTY-NINE

Chloe didn't get off the train early and walk to the office as she had done previous days. She was in a hurry to get into work, and so a leisurely stroll through Soho wasn't in the cards.

She'd seen the explosion on social media the night before. Sadly, she'd only noticed after she and Helen had gone their separate ways. She didn't think it was appropriate to try to contact Helen to let her know. Besides she was the editor-in-chief, she probably already knew.

It seemed that everyone was rallying behind *Honey Magazine*. They were trending on Twitter, Facebook users were reposting old *Honey* content, and the number of Insta-gram followers on the *Honey* account was increasing every hour. She wondered if Rose kept an eye on things during the evening, she supposed she did. Social media never slept.

She knew the feeling. She'd hardly slept either. Of course, the weather was partly to blame, but the excitement was mainly what had kept her awake. The exhilaration of having been with Helen, accompanying her to the podcast. And the jokey conversation they'd had on the way back to the train station.

Of course, she had spent a fair amount of time devastated by the geeky wave she offered to Helen from the opposite platform before Helen's train had called into the station and removed her from sight. She had no idea why she waved. Helen had softly nodded her head, a small smirk gracing her lips.

But today was a new day, and Chloe was eager to get to work. Despite how awful it had been the day before, now she was genuinely walking in as the hero she wanted to be. Okay, so she had Helen to thank for it, but she still maintained that without her original interference, none of this would've happened. And it wasn't really her fault anyway, it was Eloise Hayward's. Not Helen's, Chloe told herself. Helen was an innocent party.

A small part of her wanted to believe that she had indeed saved *Honey*. Dad would be so proud. Not that she'd share her theory with anyone in the office. They wouldn't understand.

And so, she hurried to get into the office, remaining on the Tube and encountering more armpits and body odour than was suitable for eight o'clock in the morning. Had no one heard of showers?

As she walked the short distance from the Tube station to the office, she detected someone walking in her shadow. She slowed down and tilted her head, noticing Natasha walking just behind her.

"Good morning," Chloe said brightly.

Natasha offered her a small smile and nodded her head. She almost looked like she was impressed.

"Good job," she said.

Chloe was about to launch into an explanation as to how it all came about, and to talk about how close she sat to Helen as she gave her impassioned speech. But before she had the chance to say anything, Natasha headed off and walked into a shop. Not even a goodbye.

Chloe continued walking, alone. She supposed it was the most she could expect from Natasha. Technically she should be doing cartwheels. It was the first positive comment she'd really had from her boss since she started.

She couldn't believe it was still the first week. She felt like a hardened war veteran. It hadn't been the smoothest of firsts, but she survived. Surely, they couldn't sack her now.

Could they?

As she walked into the *Honey* office, Wendy jumped up from her chair, rushed around her desk, and pulled Chloe into a hug.

"You did it, you clever girl!"

"Did what?" Chloe asked.

Wendy stepped back. The smile on her face was enormous. She looked like she might burst.

"Subscriptions are up, the marketing team are getting so many calls from advertisers that they're swamped. And the working day hasn't even started yet, everyone wants to get in first! It worked, whatever that podcast thingy was, it worked."

Chloe felt a weight lift from her shoulders. She knew the podcast had been effective for the readers, but to hear it was working in a financial sense, that people wanted advertising, it was more than she could have ever hoped for.

"I mean, the first one you did was clearly rubbish," Wendy continued. "But whatever you did in this second one was much better."

Chloe nodded in silent agreement. She decided it probably wasn't worthwhile trying to explain the technicalities of podcasts to Wendy. She was already experiencing traumatic flashbacks of trying to explain it to her parents over the phone.

"Really?" she asked instead. "Already? People are actually subscribing?"

"Yes, I think the system crashed. That's probably not good news for you, is it?"

"It's not great news, but I don't deal with that side of things," Chloe admitted. "The system crash must be because so many people are trying to get onto the site at once. That's incredible."

Tess walked into reception from the office and screamed with excitement. She pulled Chloe and Wendy into a hug and started to jump up and down. Chloe jumped along with them, wondering if this was standard procedure any time anything went well. Or if perhaps the screaming and jumping was reserved only for really good news. She'd have to figure it out what was jump-worthy over the coming weeks and months.

"The phones are ringing off the hook!" Tess said.

"Oh yes," Wendy said. She pulled away from them and rushed back to her desk. She put on her hands-free headset and started taking calls.

"She is the worst receptionist I've ever known," Tess

said. She shook her head and laughed. "Well done. Well, I know Helen said it all, but if you hadn't gone that first time, she wouldn't have needed to go and try to fix it."

"Yeah, she was amazing," Chloe admitted.

"Yes, I am," Helen said she walked into reception.

Chloe coughed and looked away.

"Can I see you in my office, please, Chloe?" Helen asked.

"Yes, sure." She walked through the bullpen, terrified of what she was about to hear. Maybe she was going to be fired? She hadn't really saved the company. In fact, she had pushed it to the brink. And then Helen had to give up her evening to go and fix it.

Or maybe it was something to do with the relationship conversation. Maybe Helen was uncomfortable working with her after having had such a personal heart-to-heart. Maybe she was going to suggest they not speak of it again, to ensure Chloe was in no doubt as to who was the boss.

She passed Kim. She looked exhausted for some reason but offered her a friendly smile all the same.

In Helen's office, Chloe took a chair whilst Helen closed the door. She was still too new to the organisation, and Helen's management style, to know if closing the door was a good or a bad thing.

"As you probably heard, things are looking up," Helen said as she sat down. "I'm very pleased with the results, but *not* with how we got there."

Chloe inclined her head. Seemed that the door closing was a bad thing.

"I understand," she said.

"I need you to come to me in the future before you act

on anything like this," Helen said. "We were lucky this time. We might not be next time."

Chloe wiped her damp palms on her skirt. She quickly nodded her head. "I understand. I will never even consider doing anything like this again."

"Well, you can consider it, but maybe come and see me first. I promise I'm very approachable."

"Yes, I know that now. I'm sorry."

"Fantastic. Well, I'll let you get to work because I'm sure it's going to be a busy day," Helen said.

Chloe quickly got to her feet, thankful for the short nature of the telling off. She opened the door, but as she started across the threshold Helen called her name. She turned around.

"Just remember," Helen said, "my door is always open." She smirked.

She remembered. Chloe rolled her eyes.

Helen laughed out loud. "I'm sorry, I couldn't help it."

"Don't worry," Chloe said, "I'm sure there will be plenty more of them."

"I hope so, you're a fine addition to the team."

Chloe blushed and turned away, rushing to her desk. It wasn't the most graceful of exits, but she didn't care. At least Helen thought she was a good hire, even if it was mainly because of the added entertainment value she brought with her.

She was fairly sure the people at the accounting firm wouldn't have been as appreciative of her strange ways.

CHAPTER FORTY

FIONA'S MORNING had quickly gone to hell. As she was on her way out of the house, her iPhone had slipped from her fingers. It somehow managed to miss two carpeted rooms and instead hit the metal door bar in between the two.

Not only was the screen broken, she was also unable to make calls. And all of her text messages were dated 1 January 1970. Realising her phone was completely out of commission, she decided to stop at the Apple Store on the way into the office. The nine-year-old at the front door informed her that she wouldn't be seen without appointment, though she had soon rectified that situation with a loud lecture on exactly how much she had spent on Apple products for her business that year alone.

She left her phone with the so-called geniuses and made her way to the office. It was such a strange sensation, being out of communication. Having no idea if anyone was calling, texting, or emailing her. She realised she hadn't been uncontactable in such a way for at least the last fifteen years. It was like a part of her was missing.

But she didn't entirely dislike it. It almost felt a little bit naughty, like she was acting out. She could get used to being off the grid.

Although she would have liked to be have been able to inform people that she was running late. She wondered if her team was worried about her. Hopefully she'd get to the office before they became too concerned.

She took a deep breath and tried to calm herself. Worrying about things wouldn't make the walk to the office any faster.

As soon as she cleared her mind about being late, she started to think about the evening she was about to spend with Nicola. She still couldn't quite fathom why Nicola had invited her to the community centre. She assumed it was some devious trap, some way to make her suffer in compensation for her terrible behaviour. Maybe the children were truly horrible. Or maybe she wouldn't even be there, and Fiona would be left standing outside some community hall waiting for someone who would never show.

She sidestepped curious tourists as she walked through the heart of Leicester Square.

She had to take her mind off of the evening and focus on the day ahead.

Yesterday had been terrible. Probably one of the worst days she had experienced at *Honey* since she began. And she included the multiple miscommunications she'd had with Nicola in that assessment. That was saying something.

She was hoping for a brand-new day, putting all of yesterday's disasters behind her. She knew it was unlikely. In actuality, she suspected today would be much worse. She idly wondered if she should start looking for a new job. She should certainly start looking for a replacement for Rose, who was always going to be the first one out of the door at the first sign of trouble.

She wondered if Nicola would take pity on her and understand that she had had two very terrible days and let her off whatever torture awaited her that evening. She doubted it. Whatever it was, she probably deserved it.

She was still beating herself up about what she had said and how she had reacted. It was ridiculous. She was a full-grown woman, supposedly an adult. And yet sometimes she really couldn't recognise herself. She consoled herself by saying it was the extreme heat that had made her react so badly. She knew it was certainly a part of it.

At least the sun wasn't quite as hot that morning. Apparently, the heatwave was soon to break, bringing glorious long-missed rain. She couldn't wait. The idea of going to bed and actually being able to sleep was blissful.

She looked at her watch. Not her Apple Watch, it wasn't happy with the whole broken iPhone situation. She'd had to go back to an old watch. She quite liked the look of it: a plain white face and a classic black leather band.

New technology was really getting in the way of some fashions. While she would no longer know how many steps she had taken, or how high her blood pressure would reach after an encounter with Pippa, there was something to be said for a nice classic timepiece.

She was forty-five minutes late. It wasn't the end of the world, she was senior management after all. Her main concern was that no one would be worried about her being late and out of communication. She'd never been late, and she was fastidious about keeping her team updated on where she was.

She picked up the pace a little bit. She took the back roads, if such a thing existed in central London. They were still crammed with people. Maybe slightly quieter than the main streets, which often meant having to step off the pavement and into the road to get around people who dawdled.

London was not designed with busy people in mind. Or rather the city allowed too many people in. Maybe there should be a limit, she considered. No, sorry, not today, London is full.

She finally arrived at the *Honey* offices. She passed through the main lobby, into the elevator, and into reception as quickly as possible.

As she arrived, Wendy looked at her with a slightly curious expression.

"Are you okay, pet?"

Fiona breathed a sigh of relief. Obviously, her delayed arrival hadn't caused too much drama. She didn't know whether to be pleased, or sad that no one cared that she was so late.

"Yes, my phone chose to have a sudden interaction with the floor. Bad morning."

It was then she noticed that Wendy was beaming, not that Wendy didn't always smile. She was often happy, but this was a full-on smile. One that said that something unusual was happening.

"I take it I wasn't missed?" Fiona asked.

Wendy shook head. "No, sorry, it's been very busy here."

Fiona rolled her eyes. "So much for a quiet day." She'd been expecting another bad day, but she'd held out hope until the last moment that it wouldn't be the case.

Helen walked into reception with a stack of paperwork and handed it to Wendy. She turned and looked Fiona.

"Everything okay?" Helen asked.

"Yes, I had to take my phone to be repaired, sorry I couldn't call," Fiona replied.

Helen chuckled. "I don't think you would've been able to get through anyway."

"How so?"

Helen smiled enigmatically. "You might want to go speak to your team." She turned smartly on her heel and walked into the main office.

Fiona looked at Wendy. "What's going on?"

"Go and see for yourself," the receptionist suggested.

Fiona entered the office and walked towards the marketing bank. Everyone was on the phone. Which was unusual. Of course, they all made calls, but it was rare for them to all be on the phone at the same time. And it was very rare that everyone was smiling as they seemed to be now. Darcy was the first to make eye contact with her. She grinned and nodded her head in greeting.

Something is going on, Fiona realised.

She sat at her desk and woke the computer up. She typed in her password and was stunned to see over one hundred unread emails that were new that morning. The red light from her phone indicated voicemails. She picked up her phone and pressed the button to access the messages. The mechanical female voice informed her that she had twenty-three voicemails waiting. She slammed the phone down again. She didn't have time to listen to them, not before she worked out what was going on.

Rose hung up a call and turned to Fiona. "Did you hear the podcast?"

Fiona shook her head. "What podcast?"

She had sworn off the idea of podcasts following what had happened previously.

"Helen was on the podcast last night," Rose explained. "The one Chloe had been on."

A wave of fury washed over Fiona. Why did people keep going on podcasts? Had no one learnt their lesson? And why didn't they tell her before they did? She was the head of marketing after all.

"She was incredible!" Rose continued. "Now everybody wants to advertise. Plus, the hashtag 'save *Honey*' is trending on Twitter. Social media in general has exploded. It started last night, I was up most of the night trying to deal with it. Digital are reporting huge numbers of sales of back issues, and new people signing up."

Fiona didn't know what to say. Within a couple of seconds, she had gone from angry at not knowing that Helen had gone on a podcast, to relieved that it seemed to have worked out. She glanced at the subject lines of her emails. Most of them seemed to be positive, a few congratulations, some requests for advertising press packs.

"I'm swamped," Lucy commented as she came off the phone. "I hope it's okay, I had to get Darcy and Rose to help me out."

"Of course," Fiona said. "Not a problem."

Out of the corner of her eye, she noticed Pippa walking towards the marketing desks. She tried to keep her eye-rolling to a minimum. Pippa hated the very concept of marketing and wasn't afraid to say so. Frequently. Her ambling over to the marketing team was rarely a good thing, even on a good-news day.

"So," Pippa began as she sidled up to the desks. "I hear good old-fashioned grassroots activism is going to be what saves *Honey*."

"Well, that and selling ad space, and copies of the magazine," Fiona added. "You know, to make money. Dirty, corporate greed."

"If you say so. I just think that it's good to see our community getting back to its roots. There are so many things that we could fight back on. I miss a good march," Pippa said.

"I bet you do," Fiona said. "I really sorry, Pippa, unless there's something you need, I'm afraid I have to crack on. There's a lot of calls to take, as I'm sure you can see."

"Of course, but if you need some words of wisdom to speak to the twittering masses, you know where I am. I don't mind admitting that I can ignite a spark into a crowd."

Pippa returned to her desk. Rose looked at Fiona with fear in her eyes.

"Please don't let her on Twitter. I've worked hard to give *Honey* a voice, and I don't want it to be replaced with hers. You can just imagine what she'd say." Rose shuddered.

"Yes, I *can* imagine," Fiona said. "I'm also well aware that the second she *looks* at Twitter, she'll be quite overcome and decide against the whole thing."

Lucy and Rose's phones started to ring at the same time. They answered their calls at the same moment that Darcy was finishing up hers. Darcy lowered the phone and walked around the desks to stand by Fiona so she didn't have to shout across them.

"I typed up a copy of the interview for you," Darcy said. "I didn't think you'd have a chance to listen to it this morning. It's all quite basic stuff, but you probably need to know what Helen said."

"You're a lifesaver," Fiona said.

Darcy smiled. "Did you have a meeting this morning?"

"No, just dropping my phone off at the Apple Store. It had a meeting with a metal floor."

"Ah," Darcy said. "Well, if you need me to go get it for you later, just let me know."

"I think I might take you up on that, it looks like I'm going to have a busy day." Fiona scrolled through her emails, wondering where to begin.

"Very busy," Darcy agreed. "But still better than yesterday."

"Tess setting fire to the office again would still be better than yesterday," Fiona mumbled, flexed her fingers, and got started.

CHAPTER FORTY-ONE

When Darcy had delivered Fiona's phone, fresh from repairs, a text from Nicola was waiting for her with a time and address for their meet-up that evening.

The day had been long and exhausting, but the good kind. There was something enormously satisfying about a productive day, especially one that followed such a gloomy day. Fiona had briefly toyed with the idea of calling Nicola and pleading for a rain check, but she'd quickly decided that it was probably best to get it over and done with.

She walked from the underground station to the community centre, just a five-minute walk according to Nicola's instructions. Dark clouds loomed in the sky, and Fiona hoped that Nicola was accurate. She didn't want to be caught out in what looked to be a heavy downpour.

She still wasn't sure why she was there, what Nicola's plan was. It wasn't like Fiona could offer any help, she was useless with kids. Kids, like dogs, could sense fear. And

Fiona feared them greatly. They were easy to break, cried on a whim, and required constant care and attention.

If Nicola was under the impression that Fiona would spend a couple of hours with some children and suddenly vow to devote all her free time to volunteering, she had another thing coming. Fiona believed in charity, of course. She knew she was extremely lucky to be born into the opportunities she had been given. Yes, she'd worked hard in university and later in her career, but she was also aware that hard work alone didn't amount to success.

But Fiona's idea of helping people was the donating kind. She wasn't the kind of person who could serve food in a soup kitchen, or someone who could run a marathon in the name of cancer research. She, like many others, was one of the cheque-writing variety of do-gooders. Armchair charity work was as far as she could manage.

Not tonight, though. Tonight, she was going to be in the thick of things. She only hoped Nicola wasn't intending to throw her into the deep end.

She entered the car park of the community centre. It was a run-down, old building, one she usually wouldn't have given a second look.

"You actually came," Nicola called out.

She turned around and saw Nicola walking towards her, a bag slung over her shoulder and her motorcycle helmet under her arm.

"I did," she agreed. "I'm still not sure why I'm here, but a deal is a deal."

Nicola stopped in front of her. "I'll make you another deal."

Fiona folded her arms. "Oh, yes?"

"You came, which many people wouldn't," Nicola said. "If you want to go, you can leave now and have your Friday evening back. Go and do whatever it is you do on a Friday night. Not clubbing as we ascertained earlier, watching the *Antiques Roadshow,* perhaps."

Fiona frowned. "You just wanted to see if I'd come?"

Nicola shrugged. "No, I'd like you to come inside and see what we do here and get involved. But I'm giving you the option to go home, if you'd like. You've shown that you're willing, but if you want to go, then that's fine. I'll still come back to *Honey.*"

Fiona couldn't fathom what Nicola's game was. Had she just dragged her halfway across London as a joke? Was she genuinely offering for her to get her evening back?

"And if I don't want to leave now?" Fiona didn't even know why she was asking. The smart thing to do would be to go home, get her heels off her aching feet, and binge-watch the new Nordic noir show she'd seen on Netflix a few weeks earlier.

Nicola smiled brightly. "Do you want to stay?"

"I don't know what I want," Fiona admitted. She looked around the car park. There were people milling around, parents and children. She was intrigued to find out what went on, and to spend some more time with Nicola. So far, she'd managed to avoid disaster. Maybe her luck was changing when it came to communicating with the photographer.

Nicola chuckled. "Well, I hope you figure it out soon. It's about to rain." She turned around and walked towards the main entrance.

Fiona looked around for a moment, chewing the inside

of her cheek. She really wanted to go home, she was so tired. But then she said she'd come, and she wanted to know more. Nicola intrigued her, and the opportunity to spend some quality time with her was one that wouldn't come up again.

"Okay, I'm coming," she called after Nicola.

Nicola slowed down and threw a smile over her shoulder.

This woman will be the death of me, Fiona thought.

Fiona wasn't great at identifying how old children were. If she had to guess, she'd say the group surrounding Nicola were between four and seven. But she'd not be surprised if she was informed that her guess was completely wrong. Really, she made it her mission to avoid children. Not because she didn't like them. She was just worried they wouldn't like her.

Nicola was perched on a tiny wooden stool, one clearly made for children. Around her were fifteen eager-looking faces.

"So, what did we talk about last time? Anyone remember?" she asked.

Hands shot up in the air. One boy in particular looked like he'd suffer an aneurism if he didn't get picked.

"Charlie?" Nicola asked, pointing to the boy.

"Shadows!"

"That's right. Shadows, sometimes called light and shade," she said. "Can anyone remember why light and shade are important?"

All hands lowered. A small girl at the front of the group tentatively raised her hand.

"Callie?" Nicola asked.

"Because you need to know where the sun or the lights are, so you can take good pictures?"

"That's right. You wouldn't want to take a really good picture, and no one can see it because it was too dark, would you?"

All the children murmured their agreement.

Nicola reached into her bag and pulled out some large prints to show to the group. As she went through the photos, she explained where the light was coming from and how it affected the picture. The pictures were of animals, playgrounds, balls, teddy bears, and landscapes. Nicola asked questions, and the group attempted to answer.

"Hi." One of the mothers had approached Fiona.

"Hello."

"I don't think I've seen you here before?" she said.

"I'm with Nicola, just helping out," Fiona said.

"Ah, I see. I'm Annie's mum, Julie."

Annie the troublemaker, Fiona thought, *if Nicola was telling the truth.*

Fiona shook her hand and introduced herself.

"Nic's great with the kids, they love her," Julie said. "And it's good because things like light and shade will come up in KS2 soon."

"Really?" Fiona was surprised. She'd never learnt about light and shade when she was at school. Admittedly, that had been some time ago.

"Yes, part of science, as well as art," Julie explained. "But it won't be as much fun as this when they learn it in school.

Plus, they get to apply being creative to science here. They learn that the two complement each other. When I was at school we were told it was either-or, but it's not really like that anymore, is it?"

Fiona hummed. She wasn't sure, she'd never given it much thought. Nicola was busy helping the children make shadow puppets with their hands and the aid of a desk lamp. She had to admit, it was an adorable sight.

"Would you mind helping me plate up some food for the kids?" Julie asked.

"Sure." Fiona had expected to be roped into something. Plating up food seemed like quite a simple task and Julie was nice enough.

She was starting to see the appeal of the community centre. The building may have been in need of a lick of paint from the outside, but inside was another matter. The rooms were decorated in bright colours and full of life.

A few of the other parents helped to set up the food for the kids. Fiona made polite small talk with them, all the while listening to Nicola's lesson. It was a world away from her workday at *Honey*. She'd gone from happily informing Helen that all ad space in the next two issues were fully booked to opening packs of chicken bites and putting them on paper plates.

Once Nicola was finished with her practical lesson, the kids started to eat. She packed away some things and walked over to where Fiona was standing.

"So? What do you think?"

"You were right," Fiona said, eyes trained on a small girl. "Annie is a troublemaker, she's claiming she doesn't eat meat, but I saw her eat a sausage roll."

Nicola laughed. "Yeah, she's a pain. Reminds me of myself when I was growing up."

"I bet you were an angel," Fiona said.

"Not really. My parents were very determined that I'd become an engineer, like my father. They knew the business, knew it would be a stable income for me, and knew I could work with Dad." Nicola leaned against the wall. "Thing was, I didn't want to be an engineer. I had this passion inside me to be creative. But engineering is about the least creative profession you can be in."

"Looks like you won the argument?" Fiona asked.

"Sort of," Nicola said. "I changed my college subjects without telling my parents. I hid my coursework from them for ages, then one day they found out. Instead of doing advanced mathematics and engineering, I was taking art, creative writing, and photography."

Fiona's jaw dropped. "That must have been a bad day."

"They threatened to kick me out of the house unless I changed my studies. Which I did," Nicola explained. "I worked hard, finished the courses and qualified to get into engineering school. Then I ran away from home, got a job at a fast-food restaurant, and lived in a house share. Eight of us in a four-bedroom house. I was like Harry Potter, living under the stairs."

Fiona couldn't imagine. Her parents hadn't been very happy when she'd come out, and there had been a couple of silent evenings at the dinner table. But they had never argued worse than that.

"I worked two jobs during the day," Nicola explained. "From very early to around dinner time. Then I attended a college that ran free courses on art most evenings. I didn't care what they were teaching, I just wanted to be able to learn about art."

Nicola took Fiona's arm in her hand and pulled her out of the main room and into the corridor. Fiona frowned and looked at her questioningly once they were alone.

"The day we fought... I was helping Chloe because that's what I do. A lot of people miss out on the opportunity to learn about art at school, or college. They are so tied up with learning a trade to get a job, they don't even think about that creative output that we all need."

Nicola huffed and ran a hand through her hair. "I overreacted because it's so important to me that people get a chance when it comes to art. People gave up their time to teach me when I was young, and I had nothing, and my hair smelt of grease from working eight-hour shifts in shitty restaurants. I made a promise to myself there and then that if I ever made something of my life, I'd give that time back and more. I'd do whatever I could to help others find that creativity. I know you feel you need to apologise to me, but I need to apologise to you as well. I overreacted, and hopefully now you understand some of why."

Fiona reached up and played with her necklace. Her mind raced. Nicola was offering *her* an apology, and an explanation?

"You have nothing to apologise for," Fiona insisted. "I was completely in the wrong, I take full responsibility. I see there were extenuating circumstances in the way you reacted, but clearly it was me who was wrong and not you."

There was a blush on Nicola's cheeks. "I just needed to be honest and explain. That kind of reaction, it's not like me."

"We were both having an off-day," Fiona agreed.

"I never would have really left *Honey*. I love working for you girls," Nicola admitted.

Fiona laughed. "So why did you go through all of this and make me come here?"

"Isn't it obvious?" Nicola asked. Her eyes shone brightly, her expression was intense.

Fiona stared at her. Her lungs felt like they might burst at the sudden change in atmosphere. "No?" she whispered.

Nicola stepped forward and pressed a soft kiss to Fiona's cheek.

"Nic?" Someone called out from the main room.

"Sorry. Duty calls," Nicola murmured before leaving Fiona alone in the empty corridor.

Fiona licked her dry lips. Her legs trembled. She was glad Nicola had left so she could have her mini-breakdown in private.

Nicola hadn't asked her to the community centre to punish her. She'd asked her so she could apologise and explain what she saw as her own overreaction. Fiona was honoured that Nicola would share something that was seemingly very private and clearly still very raw. Not to mention that kiss, which Fiona was reeling from.

"There you are," Julie said as she peeked her head into the corridor.

"Here I am," Fiona replied shakily.

"I was wondering if you would mind helping the kids with the art project. The scissors are pretty blunt, but that doesn't stop some of them from trying to cut their hair."

"Of course," Fiona agreed. She walked back towards the main room.

When she got inside, her eyes immediately sought out Nicola's. She was in conversation with a couple of parents but looked at Fiona and smiled, a light blush touching her fair cheeks. Fiona returned the smile, pleased that she wasn't the only one nervous about this new step in their relationship.

Fiona wanted nothing more than to rush over and ask what it all meant. What had just happened, what might happen next? But now wasn't the time.

"Will you help me with my stickers? I need an adult."

She looked down to see a little boy staring up at her. He held a sheet of stickers in his pudgy hands.

"Um. Sure."

He took her hand and led her across the room towards a table. She glanced up and saw Nicola grinning.

It can wait, she told herself. *We've waited this long.*

CHAPTER FORTY-TWO

"To your first full week!" Darcy raised her glass towards Chloe.

"The first full week," Rose, Lucy, and Kim chimed in.

Chloe raised her glass. Drinks softly clinked over the table, and everyone took a sip.

"I mean, we didn't think you'd get here," Darcy joked. "Considering you were trying to get yourself fired by Wednesday."

Chloe laughed along and held up her hands. "Yeah, I made some mistakes."

"I was nearly made redundant," Lucy added.

"To be fair, babe, you were going to be made redundant before Chloe put her foot in it," Kim said.

"Yeah." Rose looked up from her phone. "In fact, Chloe saved your ass, so you need to buy her another drink, pronto." She quickly lowered her head back to her phone. No one knew if she was still working on *Honey*'s social media, or if it was personal.

"You're right, I do." Lucy stood up. "Another of the same?" She pointed to Chloe's rum and coke.

"Yes, please," Chloe said.

Lucy took a quick drinks order from the rest of the table before heading off to the bar. Kim watched her girlfriend go with the look of someone truly besotted.

"Looking forward to moving in together?" Chloe asked.

Word had spread around the office fast that Lucy and Kim were taking their relationship to more solid ground. Chloe was happy for them, they seemed to be a good fit.

"I can't wait," Kim admitted gleefully. "I mean, we don't know where that will be yet. I think we've ruled out all of London, Essex, and Surrey at the moment."

"You need to lower your expectations," Darcy said.

"That's easy for you to say, you don't need to look at the price tag when looking at where you're going to live." Kim playfully elbowed her in the side.

Chloe had gotten the impression that Darcy had money, or maybe her family did.

"Of course I do," Darcy denied. "Maybe not as much as some people, but just like you, I can't live where I want."

"In Celia's house," Rose quipped without looking up from her phone.

Chloe and Kim laughed hard at Darcy's deep blush. Darcy reached across the table and ran her finger over Rose's phone screen, causing chaos to whatever she might have been doing.

"Hey!" Rose looked up and gave her a good-humoured glare.

"So," Kim looked at Chloe. "You'll be back on Monday?"

"Absolutely, wouldn't miss it," Chloe said. It was true. It had been a week of more ups and downs than she could remember in a long time. But *Honey* was starting to feel like home, and the people around the table like her family.

"Good, Pippa wants to talk to you about the new digital subscriptions," Kim said.

Chloe rolled her eyes and chuckled. "Ah, Pippa, the one reason why I might *not* come back on Monday."

"We've all been there," Rose agreed.

Lucy returned with a tray of drinks. "All been where?" she asked before sitting herself in Kim's lap.

"Dealing with Pippa," Darcy said.

"Say no more," Lucy said with a grimace. She turned and kissed Kim. "Missed you."

Darcy looked at Chloe and rolled her eyes. "I feel queasy."

"It's sweet," Chloe said.

Suddenly a loud rumble of thunder sounded from outside the pub. The skies opened, and heavy blobs of rain splattered down onto the windows. Everyone in the pub cheered boisterously, raising glasses in a toast to the storm that had been brewing all day. As much as everyone loved the sun, they were also relieved that the intense heatwave had finally broken.

Chloe tore her eyes from the windows and noted that Kim and Lucy were still kissing, unaware of the celebration going on around them.

"I want that," she said to Darcy as she pointed at the two lovebirds.

"Me too," Rose chimed in.

Kim and Lucy finally broke their lip lock and had the

decency to look embarrassed at losing themselves in such a personal moment in such a public space.

"Not seeing anyone at the moment?" Darcy asked.

"No."

"Eye on someone?" Darcy looked at her knowingly. Chloe wouldn't have been surprised if Darcy could detect a kindred spirit. At the start of the week she had almost pitied Darcy for her crush. Now she was in the same boat, thankfully with her gaze on a different older woman.

"Maybe," she allowed.

The table erupted in a series of questions and wolf whistles. Chloe felt heat rising from her cheeks. She held up her hands to quieten everyone down, to no avail.

Yes, she had found her new family. Not blood but chosen. Just like she had always hoped when she had first picked up a copy of *Honey* magazine all those years ago.

THE END

I sincerely hope you enjoyed reading Climbing the Ladder.

If you did, I would greatly appreciate a short review on your favourite book website.

Reviews are crucial for any author, and even just a line or two can make a huge difference.

SIGN UP

Every month I run a competition and randomly select three subscribers from my mailing list to win free eBooks. These books can be from my back catalogue, or one of my upcoming titles.

To be in with a chance of winning, and to hear more about my upcoming releases, click the link below to subscribe to my mailing list.

http://tiny.cc/ctl

ABOUT THE AUTHOR

A.E. Radley is an entrepreneur and best-selling author living and working in England.

She describes herself as a Wife. Traveller. Tea Drinker. Biscuit Eater. Animal Lover. Master Pragmatist. Annoying Procrastinator. Theme Park Fan. Movie Buff.

When not writing or working, Radley indulges in her third passion of buying unnecessary cat accessories on a popular online store for her two ungrateful strays whom she has threatened to return for the last seven years.

Connect with A.E. Radley
www.aeradley.com

ALSO BY A.E. RADLEY

THE ROAD AHEAD

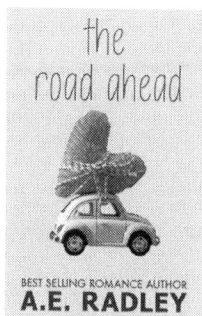

Two women from very different backgrounds. Forced to share a long journey home. Will they work together or pull each other apart?

Rebecca is stuck in Portugal. All planes to England are grounded and it's only two days until Christmas.

Desperate to get home but without money to hire a car; she's stuck. She sees an opportunity when she meets a snobby businesswoman with a broken leg, a platinum credit card, and a desire to get home. A tentative agreement is struck in order reach their destination before the festive deadline. Will they make it, or will they kill each other along the way?

A heartwarming enemies to lovers romance with a twist. Discover The Road Ahead and make your own journey home today.

BEST SELLING ROMANCE AUTHOR
A.E. RADLEY

THE ROAD AHEAD | PREVIEW

BY A.E. RADLEY

"EXCUSE ME! SORRY!"

Rebecca rushed past an elderly couple. She looked at her watch and started to run towards the terminal building. Time was running out. She had to catch her flight, she couldn't afford to miss it. Around the corner, she almost collided with another elderly couple.

Apparently, the Algarve was full of them. Slowly meandering around, not caring if they were in the way. Usually appearing to be in a world of their own. They eyed her with confusion, probably wondering what the fuss was about. The concept of time seemed to be lost on most of them.

"Sorry!" she called over her shoulder as she sidestepped them and sprinted towards the airport entrance.

She knew she shouldn't have relied on the taxi service her hotel recommended. It seemed a little too much of a coincidence that the lazy receptionist shared a surname with the taxi driver. When he'd finally turned up, he seemed less interested in getting to the airport and more interested in his telephone call. So much so that they missed the turn to the airport, adding to the delay.

The automatic doors parted, and she entered the building. She slowed her running to a jog, looking around in confusion. The departures terminal was packed with people standing around. Angry-looking people. Arms were folded, and a combined murmuring of displeasure filled the air. Something was definitely up.

Rebecca took a few steps forward and looked up at the ceiling monitors. Her eyes widened. Each and every flight on the departure board was marked as delayed.

"No, no, no," she whispered to herself.

A businessman was standing beside her, looking at his phone and shaking his head.

Rebecca turned towards him. "Excuse me, do you know what's happening?"

He looked up. "Some massive computer failure. Knocked out air traffic control in all of Portugal and Spain. Everything is grounded."

Rebecca swallowed. "Everything?" She removed her heavy backpack and lowered it to the floor.

He nodded. "Yeah, speak to a check-in assistant, but that's what they told me." He held up his phone for her to see the screen. "And that's what the news says."

"Did they say how long it would be?" Rebecca felt cold fear grip at her. She had to get home, she didn't have time for delays.

"No idea, could be ten minutes, could be ten hours. Personally, I don't think it will be that long. It can't be." He lowered his phone and gestured to the growing crowd. "This close to Christmas, they'll be calling everyone in to get it sorted out."

Rebecca looked around at the people in the departure hall. In her mind, people and planes were like water and glasses. Water spilt from a glass always looked like so much more compared to water contained in one. It was the same with people. Sat on a plane, the number of people looked reasonable, but sprawled out in an airport, they seemed like enough to fill hundreds of flights.

She turned back to the businessman. He looked authoritative, some kind of higher-up executive, she assumed. In her experience, people like that didn't always have the best grasp on reality. They assumed that their personal assistant, faithful Marjorie, would fix everything in a jiffy. They didn't know that Marjorie had sold her kidneys, killed a man, and bribed law officials to do what needed to be done because she had a large mortgage, three children, and a beagle, and needed her job whatever the cost.

"Thanks," she said. She picked up her bag and made her way through the crowds to the check-in desks.

The long row of desks was manned by exhausted-looking staff who seemed to be struggling to maintain a customer-facing smile. Luckily, there were no queues. Most people had given up speaking to the airline staff and were now standing around looking discontent, delivering filthy looks to any staff member who made eye contact.

Hoping against hope, Rebecca walked towards a free desk.

"Hi, Rebecca Edwards," she introduced herself to the woman. She took her passport and her boarding pass from her pocket and handed them over. "I'm due to fly to Heathrow, but I hear there is a delay?"

"All flights are delayed at the moment. There is a computer problem and no flights can land or take off." The woman didn't even make a move to pick up her passport or boarding pass.

"Right," Rebecca said. She chewed her lip. "Any idea of time?"

"As soon as we hear anything, it will be announced over the speaker and on the screens." The woman pointed up towards the screens that hung from the ceiling.

"Okay…" Rebecca knew that there was nothing more to be done, but she couldn't bring herself to walk away from the desk. She lowered her heavy bag to the floor again, her mind racing as she wondered what to do next.

The illogical part of her felt that standing around the check-in desk would somehow help her predicament. The desk was a critical part in the whole boarding process. Somehow, being there gave her hope. But in her heart, she knew it was futile.

"I'm sorry, there really is nothing I can do." The check-in assistant offered an apologetic smile.

"I really need to get home," Rebecca said. She leaned on the high check-in desk, pushing aside a stand-up marketing message regarding the airline's award-winning customer service. "When do you think the next plane will leave?"

"I'm sorry, but I don't have any information to give you." The assistant, Beatriz if her nametag was to be believed, tapped some buttons on her keyboard while squinting at the screen.

"I know it's not your fault," Rebecca added.

She watched as an irate German woman yelled at the poor check-in assistant beside her. She'd never understand how someone could be so mean, especially to the people on the front line. Yes, the airport had a massive computer failure. Yes, planes were grounded. Yes, it was the twenty-third of December. But that was no reason to take it out on the minimum wage check-in assistants.

"Sorry about all the people shouting at you, it must really suck," Rebecca said. She knew she didn't have to apologise for someone else's behaviour, but she wanted to.

The German woman left, blasting out obscenities as she went.

"It is a busy time of year," Beatriz replied. "Many people want to get home. The air traffic control systems have been down since early this morning, and we have no idea when they will be back up and running. It isn't just Faro Airport that's affected, it's many airports throughout the country. And in Spain, too."

"Must be horrible for you to have to deal with it," Rebecca sympathised. She fretted with her hair tie. She couldn't imagine having to tell hundreds of irate passengers that news, over and over again.

"In all my years of flying, I've never seen such incompetence!"

Rebecca winced at the British voice. She turned to look at who had taken over from the German woman to be in the running for rudest passenger of the morning.

The woman was approximately in her forties and wore a black skirt suit. Her long, blonde hair was perfectly styled in soft curls that fell to her shoulders. Rebecca glanced down at the woman's feet, noting a plaster cast on one foot, which looked at odds with the business attire. For a brief second, she wondered what had happened and felt a pang of sympathy towards her.

"I need to get back to London, now. How are you going to make that happen?" the woman demanded. She smacked her passport onto the check-in desk.

Rebecca's eyes widened at the tone. Her sympathy at the woman's cast evaporated. She turned back to Beatriz.

"Wow," she whispered and tilted her head towards the loud woman. "Rude."

Beatriz smiled and nodded in agreement.

"Don't know why she's complaining, she should fly her broom home," Rebecca muttered.

Beatriz chuckled. She looked thoughtfully at Rebecca for a moment. She leaned forward, gesturing for Rebecca to do the same.

Rebecca stood on her tiptoes and pivoted forward. She wondered why airport check-in desks were often so high. She was hardly short, but even she struggled to see over them sometimes.

"There were two planes to London due before yours," Beatriz explained, gesturing around the busy airport.

Rebecca turned around. She regarded the angry passengers standing around, most of them shaking their heads. The occasional tut could be heard.

"I can't say when the computer system will be up and running, but even if it sprang to life right now, the two planes from this morning would take priority. We don't have enough planes to take everyone today, and we can't divert from other airports as it's so close to Christmas."

Rebecca's heart rate picked up as she began to under-stand the reality of the situation.

"All of the other airlines will be fully booked," Beatriz concluded.

"You're telling me that my chance of getting home for Christmas is bad, right?" Rebecca guessed.

Beatriz nodded. "By plane, yes."

Rebecca frowned. "Is there another way? What about the trains?"

"Altogether impractical, miss. To travel from Faro to London, you would have to get to Lisbon, then take a night train to the Spanish-French border. Then, you'd have to switch to travel to Paris, and then switch again for the high-speed rail to London." The assistant frowned as if to empha-sise her point. "A lot of transfers, and it could be expensive."

Rebecca's heart sank. "Not to mention the timing. I'd never get home for Christmas."

Something about her plight must have resonated with Beatriz. The woman gestured for Rebecca to come a little closer. She did the best she could, standing on the very tips of her Converse All-Stars. "Very soon, these people are going to realise that time is running out, and they are going to look for alternative methods of transport. You can, tech-nically, drive to London and get home for Christmas. But there will be a limited number of cars available for hire…"

The penny dropped. Rebecca slowly nodded as she understood. Beatriz smiled, picked up Rebecca's passport and boarding pass, and handed them back to her.

"I'm sorry, Miss Edwards, there's nothing I can do," she said loudly.

"Thank you, thank you so much," Rebecca whispered as

she grabbed the items and hoisted her rucksack onto her shoulder.

"You better hurry," Beatriz advised quietly.

"I will, thank you again," Rebecca said. She turned and looked at the airport signage, searching for a pictogram of a car and her way home.

BRING HOLLY HOME

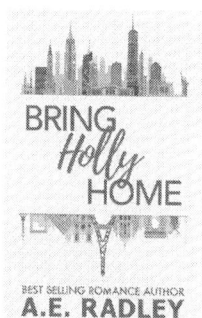

She's lost everything. Can one woman bring her home?

Leading fashion magazine editor Victoria Hastings always thought that her trusted assistant quit her job and abandoned her in Paris.

A year later, she discovers that Holly Carter was injured in an accident. Brain trauma led to amnesia and Holly cannot remember anything about her life.

Guilt causes Victoria to bring Holly home and into her life to aid her in recovery. But when guilt turns into something else, what will she do?

BRING HOLLY HOME | PREVIEW

BY A.E. RADLEY

LOUISE TOOK a deep breath and quickly started to recite the schedule to her boss.

"So, as you know, the gala is tonight. The table plan is in your room for final approval as you requested. Your car arrives tomorrow at ten o'clock to take you to Charles de Gaulle. I'll be checking out of the hotel earlier to get the Guerlain samples that you requested for your sister, so I'll meet you at the airport at quarter to eleven."

Louise knew this was an exercise in futility. Her boss knew the schedule back to front, and yet she felt the urgent need to fill the awkward silence that permeated the back of the limousine. She subtly turned her wrist in her lap to look at her watch.

"Hm," Victoria murmured.

Louise looked up to see if her boss would say anything else.

Victoria continued to look over the top of her glasses at the passing Parisian scenery.

Louise debated if she should say something else. Maybe give another rundown on the first-class menu on offer on-board the flight from Paris to New York. Maybe attempt to get a tiny amount of kudos for having changed the red meat option from lamb for the entire cabin, simply because Victoria couldn't abide the smell of lamb.

Not that Victoria would ever acknowledge any of the backbreaking, soul-destroying work that Louise did on a daily basis for the impossible-to-please woman. But she lived in hope that a nugget of gratitude would work its way into Victoria's conscience.

Maybe enough to promote her from her role of assistant. Being an assistant to Victoria Hastings was certainly prestigious. Sadly, it didn't pay the therapy bills that Louise would need if she managed to survive the role.

Louise's mobile phone rang, and she answered immediately. "Yes?"

It was that awful French man from the gazette again. Blathering on about something or other and making little sense.

"Look, I've told you before, Victoria will not be doing any interviews. If you wanted to speak to her then you should have called *before* she arrived in Paris for Fashion Week. Do you have any idea how busy she is? Of course you don't."

The man continued talking hurriedly. Louise just shook her head, not even bothering to listen to what he was saying. She couldn't believe the audacity of the man. Thinking that Victoria Hastings of all people would be able to drop everything and speak to some nobody. Did he have any idea who she was?

"Absolutely not, and don't call this number again!"

Louise huffed, hung up the phone, and tossed it into her bag.

"Damn French," she mumbled under her breath.

"Problem?"

Louise looked up and realised that Victoria had turned to glance at her. Louise took pride in her appearance, checking her reflection at least every twenty minutes to ensure she was looking her best. But the second Victoria looked at her, she felt certain that she must appear a wreck.

Victoria was the kind of woman who always looked perfect. She must have had a long conversation with Mother Nature in which she put her foot down and insisted she wasn't going to age another minute. And so, forty-seven-year-old Victoria Hastings looked like a perfectly turned-out woman in her mid-thirties. Not a hair was out of place in her fashionable blonde bob. Her makeup was light but always on point, just enough to rouge her cheeks, plump her lips, and accentuate her steely green eyes. Nothing less could be expected of the editor of one of the world's leading fashion magazines.

Louise realised that she had been silent for too long. Her panic at potentially not looking her best under Victoria's frosty glare had thrown her.

"Um. No, no problem, Victoria. Just a journalist, some awful little French man. You know what journalists are like. I don't even know why I bother sending out press guidelines. He has been calling me here and Claudia back in New York every single day… I… He…" Louise swallowed nervously.

She'd said too much, she'd bothered Victoria with details that were of no interest to her.

Victoria simply stared at her in silence. Slowly, she rolled her eyes. Louise was sure that Victoria was internally questioning the incompetence she was surrounded by. She usually did. Now it was just a matter of whether Victoria would deliver a softly spoken, but scathing, remark, or if she would ignore her. Louise held her breath while she waited for judgement to be passed.

After a few more frosty seconds, Victoria turned and looked out of the car window again. The conversation was over.

Louise released the breath she had been holding. Silently.

Paris Fashion Week was everything she'd hoped it would be. The shows, the designers, the clothes, the city. But now it was drawing to a close. Three months of doing nothing but planning Victoria's schedule had paid off. It had been a success. Not that anyone would know it from Victoria's expression.

From the moment they had landed in Paris, her boss has been quiet and detached. More so than usual. At the best of times, no one would ever accuse Victoria of being friendly or talkative. In fact, Victoria was famously known for destroying careers with a simple look.

But the last few days had been worse than usual.

Louise reminded herself that there was just one more night between her and her comfy bed back home in New York. And the next morning she would be getting to the airport bright and early and thankfully not travelling with Victoria.

The elevator doors slid open, and Victoria put on her over-sized Gucci sunglasses. She walked through the lobby of the Shangri-La Hotel, her heels tapping loudly on the marble flooring.

She could sense the receptionists discreetly looking at her as she walked past them. She imagined that they were breathing a sigh of relief at her departure.

The doorman, dressed in a top hat and a knee-length, forest green overcoat, opened the door as she approached. She breezed through and down the steps.

She let out an audible sigh at the fact that her limousine wasn't in place. She looked up with annoyance to see that the vehicle was on its way down the hotel's driveway, just passing through the wrought iron gates.

"Apologies, Ms Hastings."

She turned to see the manager of the hotel rushing down the steps. He waved his arms frantically to hurry the black limousine up. The moment it came to a stop in front of the steps, he opened the back door and gestured into the car.

"Thank you for your stay. I do hope you found everything to your liking?"

Victoria hummed half-heartedly. While the Shangri-La was slightly above average in some respects, there had been some issues. For starters, the intolerable noise of the fan in her room and the maintenance imbecile who said he couldn't even hear the noise when she had been positively deafened by it.

She passed the grovelling man and got in the back of the limo.

"We do hope to see you again next year," the man continued, holding the door open and looking at her with a pleading expression.

Victoria felt that it was very unlikely that she'd ever come back should he continue to delay her. She wanted to get to the airport and take a few private moments to call her children to see how they were doing. She travelled a lot, but she never stopped missing them.

She was about to instruct the driver to go, regardless of the position of the passenger door, when she noticed the manager looking up the driveway with a frown. She could hear some kind of commotion from behind the car.

"*Excusez-moi,* Madame Hastings!"

She glanced out of the back window. A scruffy-looking man was running towards the car. It looked like he had run through the gates as they were being closed. He held up a piece of paper and was running determinedly towards her. Two doormen and a security guard were chasing after him.

She turned around and called out to the driver in a bored tone, "Go."

The hotel manager closed the passenger door and the car slowly started to edge forward, the sharp turn of the driveway making a quicker departure impossible.

She heard shouts behind the car and rolled her eyes. It seemed nothing was going to go right during this trip.

There was a thump on the window. The scruffy man stood beside the car, holding up a Polaroid photograph. Victoria felt her mouth fall open in shock at the image.

It was Holly Carter. Her former assistant. The one who

had abandoned her without a word exactly one year ago. However, there were vast differences between the Holly she had known and the woman in the photograph.

In contrast to Holly's long locks, the photograph showed a woman with short hair. Victoria's artistic sensibilities balked at the change. Long hair was finally back in fashion and the girl had chopped all of hers off. Not that Holly was ever one to toe the line when it came to fashion trends.

But the real shock was the unresponsiveness in her eyes. They no longer sparkled, there was a dullness to them that Victoria had never seen before. And Holly's already pale skin seemed paler, almost sickly in appearance. The forced smile failed to distract from the fact that she looked quite frightened.

As quickly as the photograph had been slapped onto the glass, it was pulled away. Each doorman grabbed one of the scruffy man's arms and dragged him away from the car.

"Wait," she instructed the driver.

Victoria felt the brakes being applied, and the car came to a jolting stop. She opened the door and stepped out of the car.

The man was now on the tarmac, the two burly doormen on top of him, trying to hold him down. He looked up at her.

"You know her?" he asked, his voice thick with a French accent.

"Let him go," she commanded in a soft tone.

The doormen looked in confusion at the manager who was standing helplessly by. He quickly waved his hands up to indicate that they should let him go.

Slowly, the man climbed to his feet. He clutched the photo in his hand and looked at Victoria expectantly.

She looked him up and down. She had no idea who he was or what he wanted, but he seemed to know Holly. And that was enough to grant him a few moments of her time. Even if she was running late.

She pointed to the car.

"Get in," she instructed.

Published by Heartsome Publishing
Staffordshire
United Kingdom
www.heartsomebooks.com

Also available in paperback.
ISBN: 9781912684106

First Heartsome edition: August 2018

Made in the USA
Middletown, DE
18 August 2018